Miss Brown, Vol. 3

Vernon Lee

Table of Contents

Miss Brown, Vol. 3 1
    Vernon Lee 1
    BOOK VII. (Continued) 1
    CHAPTER II 2
    CHAPTER III 10
    CHAPTER IV 21
    CHAPTER V 34
    CHAPTER VI 44
    CHAPTER VII 57
    BOOK VIII 65
    CHAPTER I 65
    CHAPTER II 70
    CHAPTER III 76
    CHAPTER IV 82
    CHAPTER V 87
    CHAPTER VI 96
    CHAPTER VII 99
    CHAPTER VIII 106
    CHAPTER IX 110
    CHAPTER X 119
    CHAPTER XI 125

Miss Brown, Vol. 3

Vernon Lee

Kessinger Publishing reprints thousands of hard-to-find books!

Visit us at http://www.kessinger.net

- BOOK VII. (Continued)
- CHAPTER II.
- CHAPTER III.
- CHAPTER IV.
- CHAPTER V.
- CHAPTER VI.
- CHAPTER VII.
- BOOK VIII.
- CHAPTER I.
- CHAPTER II.
- CHAPTER III.
- CHAPTER IV.
- CHAPTER V.
- CHAPTER VI.
- CHAPTER VII.
- CHAPTER VIII.
- CHAPTER IX.
- CHAPTER X.
- CHAPTER XI.

BOOK VII. (Continued)

CHAPTER II.

WHILE Anne was being indoctrinated with her cousin's philosophical theories, Hamlin had little by little let himself be drawn into the little clique of more mystical and Bohemian pre-Raphaelites whom Edmund Lewis had collected round Madame Elaguine. The old-fashioned, long-established æsthetes, who believed that artistic salvation resided solely in themselves and their kith and kin, and who strangely muddled together the theories of an esoteric school and the prejudice of the untravelled Briton, decidedly set their face against Madame Elaguine. They had not liked Anne Brown because she was not sufficiently engaging; but they thoroughly hated Sacha Elaguine because she was too fascinating.

"A nasty, ignorant, frivolous little woman," said Mrs Spencer, who was the spokeswoman of the party; "a woman with no sense of responsibility whatever. Did you hear the way in which she spoke of those horrible French painters? That she actually dared to talk to papa about that Monsieur Page, vulgar, base creature that he is!"

And the older people, and the women of the æsthetic world—the spinsters with dishevelled locks and overflowing hearts, who kept little garlanded lamps before the photographs of puny English painters and booted and red-shirted American poets, all agreed with her. But the younger men merely laughed, and neglected the solemn, smut-engrained parlours of Bloomsbury, the chilly, ascetic studios of Hampstead, for Madame Elaguine's curious, disorderly, charming house in Kensington—the house patched up with old lodging-house furniture and all manner of Eastern stuffs and brocades, crowded with a woman's nick-nacks, strewn with French novels and poems, and redolent of cigarettes and Russian perfumes. For there was in this delicate, nervous little creature, eaten up with love of excitement, something which acted as a spell upon most men; and it was curious to see how she managed to make them all in love with her, and at the same time excite no jealousy.

"Do you think Circe's pigs were jealous of each other?" asked Mrs Spencer, when this peculiarity was pointed out to her by Chough. "Reduce people to a certain level, and they will be satisfied with equality."

Lewis explained it as being due to Madame Elaguine's magnetic power. Whether the

Russian had been fully converted to his spiritualistic theories, or, indeed, whether it was possible to make her believe seriously in anything, it is impossible to say. But she had caught the spiritualistic infection from Lewis as a tinder catches fire. Nothing in the world could suit her better: spiritualism appealed to her love of excitement and mystery, to an idealistic and mystical strain which made her hanker after strange supersensuous contacts and occult affinities; moreover, if ever there was a woman of whom one might believe that she could vibrate with disembodied passion, and come in contact with an uncorporeal world, it was this emaciated, nervous, hysterical creature, who lived off coffee and cigarettes, and lived, as it seemed, only with her restless mind, and not at all with her frail, incapable body.

"I feel sometimes," she would say to her friends, "as if I mixed with the living as smoke mingles with air—seeing them move before me, but unable to clutch them or be clutched by them, coming in contact only with their passions. I feel as if I could more easily live with the dead—mix more easily with them. It is terrible. I sometimes fancy that I shall fall in love with some dead creature, and my life be sucked away by him,"—and she gave a little shudder.

Page 7

Cosmo Chough listened spell-bound with admiration, twisting and untwisting his long black whiskers. What a woman was this! And he ruminated over a new chapter of his Triumph of Womanhood, of which Sacha Elaguine—"Sacha quite short," as she bade her friends call her—should be the heroine.

Edmund Lewis smiled his sensual lazy smile, which one knew that he imagined to be the prototype of the cruel and lustful mysterious smile of the men and women, and creatures neither one nor the other or both, who came from beneath his fantastic pencil.

"Has it never occurred to you," he said, in his luscious voice, stooping over Madame Elaguine's chair, "that you may rather be a dead creature yourself—a vampire come to suck out some one's life-blood?"

"Confound that Lewis!" thought Chough. "Why must such ideas occur to him, a mere damned painter, and not to me, who am a poet?" and he made a note of the vampire.

Hamlin was standing by, smoking his cigar-ette sullenly. He did not like these sort of liberties which Lewis took with his cousin; he had even of late warned her that, although his friend was an excellent fellow, too great intimacy with him might prove disagreeable to her.

"What a carrion-feeding fancy you have, Lewis!" he exclaimed, frowning. "One would think you lived on corpses, in order to be more in harmony with those beasts of spirits of yours."

Lewis laughed triumphantly; but Madame Elaguine, to his amazement, cut him short by saying—

"Your idea may be very amusing, Mr Lewis; but I don't think it is exactly the style of thing for a man to say to a woman."

Lewis, who was never abashed, merely raised his eyebrows.

"I thought you were superior to your sex," he answered.

"If Lewis dare to talk to you like that," whispered Hamlin to Sacha, "I shall horsewhip him one of these days."

Page 9

Madame Elaguine pressed his fingers in her little hot hand.

"You are good," she answered, in what was like the buzz of a gnat, but infinitely caressing; "but poor Lewis means no harm: he is very *bon enfant*. You are too pure and proud to understand other men. Ah, Anne is a happy woman!"

The last words were scarcely more than a little sigh to herself; but Hamlin caught them, and reddened.

"Anne is very cold," he said briefly; then added, as if to justify himself in his own eyes—"I suppose all very passionate natures are."

Sacha shook her little thin childish head.

"Oh no—not all."

Miss Brown went but rarely to the house of Hamlin's cousin. She was extremely sorry for the poor little woman's misfortunes; and asking herself what she would have been had she had Madame Elaguine's past, she often admired how the Russian had kept her independence and self-respect, and serenity and cheerfulness. Yet, while she believed herself fully to appreciate Sacha, and invariably defended her against the jealous prudery of Mrs Spencer and her clique, Anne somehow felt no desire to see much of her. She set it down to her own narrowness and coldness of temper. "I am too one-sided to have friends," she used to say to Mary Leigh; "I feel that I don't do justice enough to people, however much I try, and that my heart does not go out to meet them enough. I think I would do my best for them; but I can't love them or be loved."

Poor Mary Leigh was silent. Anne—this beautiful noble, distant, somewhat inscrutable Anne—was the idol of the enthusiastic Irish girl. She had often longed to tell her so; she longed, at this moment, to put her arms round Anne's neck, and say quite quietly—"I love you, Anne;" but she had not the courage. How much may this sort of cowardice, called reticence, cheat people of? The knowledge that there is a loving heart near one, that there is a creature whom one can trust, that the world is not a desert,—all this might be given, but is not. And the other regrets, perhaps throughout life, that word which remained unspoken, that kiss which remained ungiven, and would have been as the draught of water to the wearied traveller.

Anyhow Anne, while thinking that she liked Madame Elaguine, somehow did not care to see much of her. What she could do for her she did willingly. Madame Elaguine wanted the child to learn English, but made a fuss about letting her have a governess.

"My child's mind must be my own mind," she said. But as she went on grieving at little Helen's ignorance, and her own incapacity, from want of schooling and want of strength, to teach her, Anne offered to teach the child together with the little Chough girls, who were still her pupils. Madame Elaguine was rapturously grateful; but Helen was so completely spoilt, that she could be brought to Anne only when she fancied it herself, and Anne found her so demoralised that she really did not like to bring her in contact with the Choughs. "When poor little Helen is ten, then you must moralise her," Madame Elaguine would say; and Helen was within week of being ten, and Anne, much as she disliked asking Madame Elaguine anything, urged that she should begin to be taught. Moreover, Anne's time was too much taken up reading under Richard Brown's directions, and her thoughts were too much preoccupied to make her feel at all sociable, even had she not felt an instinctive repugnance to the sort of company, headed by Edmund Lewis, which she knew she would meet at Madame Elaguine's.

However, one evening she could not refuse Sacha's invitation, more especially as the latter, evidently to please Anne, had invited her friends the two Leighs. It was a grand spiritualistic *séance* . Madame Elaguine was in great excitement, and Edmund Lewis was radiant. But Hamlin looked bored and pressed.

"I hate all this vulgar twaddle of spiritual– ism," he said impatiently to Anne. Anne loathed it: the triviality disgusted her, the giving up of one's will to another revolted her, and she could not understand how a woman could endure to be handled and breathed upon by a man like Lewis. Mary Leigh was half excited and half amused; Marjory, the strong–minded scoffer, had determined to unmask some sort of trickery. The *séance*, to which Edmund Lewis had brought a famous professional medium, was very much like any other *séance* : a darkened room, a company of people partly excited, partly bored; expectation, disappointment, faith, incredulity; moving of tables and rapping, faint music, half visible hands.

"The whole boxful, machinery complete, all the newest tricks, eighteenpence," as little Thaddy O'Reilly fiippantly remarked to Anne. How could Madame Elaguine have patience with such rubbish? wondered Miss Brown. What excitement could that excitement–loving little woman, with a real mystery in her own life, find in all this stale shibboleth?

"You can't think what a strange, delightful sensation I have at these moments," said Sacha to Hamlin, as her little soft hand touched his. "I seem to feel the whole current of your life streaming through me, and mingling with mine. It is like an additional sense. Do you understand that, Anne?"

"No," answered Anne, briefly. "I feel Mr Hamlin's fingers touching mine, and that's all."

Hamlin somehow admired Anne's answer; he was glad it was so,—had she felt like his cousin, something would have spoilt in an ideal of his; and yet Anne's coldness annoyed him.

"The spirits are reluctant; there are too many sceptics in the room," said Edmund Lewis, angrily. "Great as is the power of some of us—as, for instance, of Madame Elaguine—I feel that there is something acting as a non-conductor,—some very chilly nature here."

But nevertheless, when the company was giving up the *séance* as spoilt, mysterious sounds were heard, and something luminous, which was immediately identified as a pair of spirit-hands, was seen to float over the table.

"Spirit-hands!" whispered Edmund Lewis.

"Wash-leather gloves painted over with luminous paint," whispered Thaddy O'Reilly.

"A wreath!" whispered Madame Elaguine.

Something round, like a wreath, did seem to float, supported by the spirit-hands. Some said it was oak, others cypress, others myrtle; but it soon became apparent that it was bay.

"For Hamlin!" whispered the guests to each other.

The wreath floated unsteadily over the heads of the party; but, as it passed Marjory Leigh, that evil-minded young materialist quickly snatched at it, but it was whisked away by the indignant spirits. There was a murmur of indignation; but indignation turned into triumph when suddenly the wreath reappeared, and hovered for two good minutes over Hamlin's head. There was a cry of admiration, and Madame Elaguine clapped her hands.

But Marjory Leigh struck a light, and lit the candle by her side. She could see faintly the excited faces all round, and among them the pale face of Anne Brown, scornful and angry, fixed upon that of Hamlin, who was flushed, hesitating, surprised.

"I am glad the spirits have such good taste in poetry," said Marjory Leigh, quietly; "but it is a pity that they should not have crowned Mr Hamlin, like Petrarch and Corinne, with real laurels." And she stretched out something in the palm of her hand. Every one crowded round, and took it up by turns.

It was a leaf, torn and broken, of green laurel which she had pulled off when the crown had passed over her; but the green laurels were masses of stamped paper, and left a green stain in the hand.

"It does smack a little of a French *pensionnat de demoiselles* distribution of prizes; you will get the little book *dorésur tranches*, 'Avec l'approbation de Monseigneur l'Archevêque de Tours,' and 'Prix décerné à M. Walter Ham– lin,' written inside, at the next *séance*," cried Thaddy O'Reilly. "Well, it is consoling to see how our beloved dead keep up the simple habits of the living."

There was a titter. Madame Elaguine burst out laughing. Hamlin laughed, but he looked black as thunder.

"You brought that piece of green paper with you!" cried Lewis furiously at Marjory Leigh. "You brought it to insult and delude us! It is disgraceful."

"My dear Lewis," said Thaddy O'Reilly, gently, "remember that you are still a gentleman, and not yet a spirit."

"Had I known that there was to be any crowning, I should certainly have brought something better than paper laurels," said Marjory, fiercely. "I never thought spirits were reduced to such expedients as these."

The *séance* came to an end. The lamps were lit. The medium dismissed with considerable contumely. Edmund Lewis went away in a huff; and Madame Elaguine, who cared in spiritualism only for those strange thrills which she had before described, laughed a great deal about the matter, and settled down to make music with Cosmo Chough.

Hamlin looked as if he wished himself a thousand miles away. He would speak with no one; he was angry with his cousin for having let him in for such a ridiculous scene, and angry with the rest of the company for having witnessed it; he had no command over his looks; and while Madame Elaguine's curious, warm, childish voice throbbed passionately through Schumann's songs, or while people took their tea and talked, he sat aside, in the doorway of the next room, like a whipped child.

"What a baby Walter is!" whispered Madame Elaguine, laughing, to Chough.

But Anne did not laugh. She felt the humiliation not of the paper laurels, but of that radiant look which she had seen in Hamlin when the lights had first been lit. And she was indignant with Hamlin for tak- ing this ridiculous business so tragically, and at the same time sorry for his poor, wounded, unsympathised-with vanity. She left the piano, where she had been sitting near Sacha, and went to him where he sat disconsolately looking over a heap of newspapers in the next room.

She did not allude to the scene. What use was it chiding him? He could never understand. She talked to him about the picture which he was painting, about the people, anything to make him feel that she was sorry for him. Hamlin was bitter against his friends; he began once more his tirades against modern art and poetry, its lifelessness and weakness; he again declared himself longing for a different life; he again, passionately and delicately, called upon Anne, in his veiled way, to redeem him. Anne listened sadly. She knew it all so well by heart, this vain talk which was to be the daily bread of her soul.

Suddenly Hamlin's eye fell upon Marjory Leigh, who was seated talking with Thaddy O'Reilly in the recess of a window.

"I wonder you can endure that girl, Miss Brown!" he cried, "much less make her your friend."

"Marjory may sometimes be rude, and it was perhaps not very good manners to interrupt the *séance* as she did, although I quite sympathise with her; but she is a capital girl, and just one of the most trustworthy persons I know."

"She is a humbug!" exclaimed Hamlin, crossly and violently. "Doesn't she set up for philanthropy, and self-sacrifice, and all that? and then she goes to parties dressed in that way—a fit beginning for the wife of an East End curate, for a man like Harry Collett!"

"Marjory's dress does not cost more than Harry Collett's coats," answered Anne, quietly. "You men never understand such things, and think because a girl's dress is showy that it is expensive. Of course Marjory doesn't wear æsthetic things, and it would be absurd if she did; but I happen to know that she made that particular dress entirely with her own hands."

"I know nothing about the dress, except that a wife of Harry Collett's should not go about like a peacock. But I do know," cried Hamlin, fiercely, "that it is disgraceful for a girl engaged to marry, and to marry a man like Harry, to sit the whole evening in a corner, letting a jackanapes like O'Reilly make love to her."

"Marjory has been sitting with Mr O'Reilly only about ten minutes," answered Anne, indignantly, "and she has known him ever since they were babies. I think it is too ridiculous if a girl can't talk to a young man at a party without being treated as if she were committing an infidelity."

"I don't say that any other girl talking to any other young man is to blame," said Hamlin, still hotly; "but I say that a woman who can let O'Reilly flirt with her throughout the evening is no wife for Collett; and I have a good mind to write and tell him so," and Hamlin looked dignified.

Anne did not answer at first. She was filled with contempt for this vain childish ill-humour, which was taking the proportions of rabid hatred.

"Marjory is my friend," she at last said, "and I think that the less you talk such nonsense as about writing to Mr Collett, the better."

"I will, upon my word!" exclaimed Hamlin. "Marjory Leigh is a friend of yours, but she is an infamous flirt all the same!"

"Why does Mr Hamlin glare at me like that?" asked Marjory of Anne a little later. "One would think it was my fault that the spirits crowned him with paper laurels and not with bay-leaves."

CHAPTER III.

ANNE had forgotten all about the *séance*, when, about a week later, Mary Leigh arrived at Hammersmith in a state of extreme excitement.

"What is the matter, Mary?" asked Anne, wondering at her flushed face, which was usually so quiet.

"Nothing—nothing," said Mary Leigh, looking impatiently at some visitors who were present. "I spoilt two copper plates this morning, and shall have no etchings worth exhibiting. I suppose that has put me out of sorts."

But the visitors had scarcely turned their backs, when Mary Leigh turned suddenly towards Miss Brown.

"Oh Anne dear, a dreadful, shameful thing has happened! and I have come to you to know what it means, because I can't help thinking that Mr Hamlin has had something to do with it, and poor Marjory is so miserable."

"What is it?" asked Anne, a vague terror coming over her.

"Why, Marjory got this letter to-day from Harry Collett; he has been staying with his mother at Wotton for the last week. Read it, and you will understand."

Miss Brown took the letter, evidently much pulled about and read and re-read, from Mary Leigh, and smoothed it out and read it slowly; while her friend sat by, looking anxiously at her face.

The letter was from Marjory's intended. Harry Collett told her, with a dignity and gentleness, a desire not to hurt the one who had hurt him, and an incapacity of hiding his great pain, which nearly made Anne cry, that his eyes had at length been opened to the undesirableness of a mar- riage which, however much wished for by him, could not satisfy all the claims of a nature llke Marjory's.

"Much as I have looked forward to our marriage," wrote poor Harry, "I could not possibly be happy if I suspected that it did not give you everything which you have a right to require from life. I thank God for having sent me a warning in time, for having let me understand what your generosity and my infatuation would have hidden to me—namely, that your thoughts have, despite your will, turned elsewhere; that your nature requires a life of greater cheerfulness and variety than I could hope to give it. And, indeed, I am beginning also to understand that I was trying to reconcile the irreconcilable—that a man who has elected a life among the poor, has no right to share its privations with any one, much less with any one dear to him; and I see that I was on the verge of committing the sin of sacrificing your happiness to my vocation, or rather to my unmanly desire to have the hardness of my vocation sweetened at your expense. Please do not fancy that I think at all badly of you; I think badly only of my own blindness."

But the poor curate's angelic nature could not resist the temptation of a fling at his supposed rival.

"I am only surprised—but my surprise may be due to my ignorance," he added, "at the person who engrosses your thoughts. I should never have thought you could seriously care for a shallow creature like O'Reilly. I wish you to be happy, but I fear you will not be solidly happy with him."

"Do you understand?" cried Mary Leigh, impatiently; "some one has written to Harry some horrid lies about Marjory and Thaddy O'Reilly. Oh, I think it is too shameful! Marjory, who has not seen Thaddy O'Reilly more than twice in the last six months; and," added Mary Leigh, with an agony in her voice, "I fear—oh, I fear—Anne, that it must have been Mr Hamlin who did it."

Anne did not look up from the letter. She was very white, and her face full of shame.

"I fear it must," she answered, half audibly.

"But what is the meaning of it?" cried Mary. "What can Mr Hamlin know about the matter? Why, he scarcely ever sees Marjory. I don't believe he had seen her for nearly six weeks before that party at Madame Elaguine's. Oh, Anne, do you think it is Madame Elaguine, that horrid little Russian, who did it?"

"Oh no," answered Anne, quickly, "I know Sacha Elaguine has not done it; I don't believe she is capable of doing it."

"Then you think? . . ."

"I fear—I fear Mr Hamlin did it."

There was a dead silence. Poor Mary Leigh was torn by her indignation for her sister, and her pain at the shame cast upon her admired Hamlin, and through him upon her adored Anne.

"What can I do? If only I knew the grounds of the accusation," she said desper– ately, "I know I could explain them away to Harry. I know that Marjory could, but she won't."

"Has Marjory not answered Mr Collett?"

Mary Leigh shook her head.

"Marjory is too proud and self-willed. She is disgusted with Harry. She won't hear his name mentioned; it is useless. Oh, it is dreadful to see people who care for each other so much separated in this way, by a mere vile groundless calumny, which one cannot even refute."

Anne passed her hand across her forehead.

"Mr Hamlin has done it," she said slowly, and with an effort, "and he must undo it."

"*How* can one make him undo such a thing?" cried Mary, hopelessly.

"I will tell him that he was wrong, and make him write to Harry Collett."

"Oh Annie dear, you are good"—and Mary Leigh threw herself on Anne's neck—"for I know how dreadful, how terrible it must be for you to tell him that he has acted badly."

"It is not the first time," answered Anne, mournfully. "Leave me the letter, will you, Mary dear?"

Mary Leigh left the letter with Miss Brown; and that evening, as Anne was sitting with Hamlin after dinner, she suddenly dashed into the subject.

"Do you remember saying, the other night, at your cousin's, that you would write to Harry Collett about the flirtation which you took it upon yourself to imagine between Marjory Leigh and Mr O'Reilly?" asked Anne.

Hamlin looked puzzled.

"I remember something or other," he said evasively.

"Did you write to Harry Collett?"

"I had occasion to write to Collett about some books I had left at Wotton, and which I wanted him to bring up to town on his return."

"But did you mention about Marjory and Mr O'Reilly?"

"I may have"—Hamlin spoke absently—"yes, I suppose I did. What of it?"

"What of it?" cried Anne, indignantly; "why, this much, that you have made two people perfectly miserable, and that Marjory's marriage with Mr Collett is broken off," and she handed him the letter.

Hamlin looked at it with an air of puzzled indifference.

"I don't understand what it's all about," he said, coolly and serenely, returning the letter to Anne.

"Then you did not say anything about Marjory to Mr Collett?"

"Yes—I did—I certainly think I did. I can't exactly remember what it was. You know how one writes letters; one forgets the next day."

Anne looked at him with wonder. So after having, momentarily at least, made two people as unhappy as was well possible, this was how he took the revelation of the results of his doings.

"Mr Hamlin," said Anne, sternly, "you know that you never believed that Marjory Leigh was really flirting with O'Reilly; and you know that you wrote to Harry Collett, and made him believe that she cared for another man."

"I don't know anything about Miss Leigh's doings. I remember noticing her talking very assiduously that evening with Thaddy. Perhaps it was all fancy of mine; I have no doubt it was. I just mentioned it to Collett as I might mention anything else. I never dreamed that it would annoy him."

"You thought it would merely annoy her?" asked Anne, reproachfully.

"I really know nothing about the matter. I'm not responsible for what I may have thought or written a week ago, much less for all these complications, which I never dreamed of."

"Did you suppose, then, that Harry Collett would be utterly indifferent to being given to understand that Marjory cared for another man, and was not the fit wife for an East End curate, as you expressed it?"

"I don't know. I wrote, and thought no more about it. If they have gone and quarrelled about it, I'm very sorry—and that's all I can say."

Hamlin's tone was bored and slightly impatient. He had evidently not the smallest shame or regret for what he had done.

"Since you are sorry—since you *did* write that to Collett," said Anne, trying to speak as gently as possible—"you will, I trust, do what you can to repair this mischief. Marjory Leigh is too indignant with Harry to answer him at all. Will you write to him and tell him that it was all a mistake—all owing to your having been annoyed with Marjory on account of that laurel crown business—and that there was no foundation for all you said? You will make amends, won't you? Do write at once."

Hamlin had risen from his seat, and his face had taken a curious obstinate look.

"I'm very sorry I can't obey you, Miss Brown," he said, "but it appears to me that you wish me to write myself down a liar. If these people choose to fall out because of a word of mine, I see no reason to apologise. It is their concern, not mine."

"Was it your concern to write to Collett, then? Was it your concern to take such a responsibility?"

"Every one may write whatever passes through his head. I thought Miss Leigh a flirt last week; I don't now. As to responsibilities, I repudiate such things."

"No one can repudiate such things," cried Anne. "You have done mischief, and with a few strokes of the pen you can repair it. Oh, you must write, Mr Hamlin—you must."

"If I write," answered Hamlin, hotly, "I shall just tell Collett that I *do* think Miss Leigh a flirt. I cannot refuse to write, but I refuse to eat my words. Have you paper and a pen?"

He had gone to Anne's writing–table. Anne put her arm over it.

"You have told a falsehood once, you shall not tell it twice," she said.

"I said that merely to show you how impossible your request was. After all, my dear Miss Brown, a man does owe something to himself and to his name, and there is such a thing as proper pride."

"Is there?" answered Anne, and the words were like drops of freezing water. "I thought," she added, the remembrance of what he had answered when she had entreated him not to slander himself in those sonnets "Desire," "that your school considered it legitimate for a man to say that he had committed no matter what baseness, even those which he had not. But I see," and Anne's indignation blazed up, "that you want sometimes to be considered wicked, but that you succeed only in being mean."

"I think that is a little hard upon me," he answered mournfully and bitterly, and left the room. He was thinking of all he had done for Anne—all that he had done and left undone.

Anne remained seated, looking into the fire, for some moments. Then she went to her desk and took paper and an envelope.

"DEAR MR COLLETT," she wrote slowly, "Mary Leigh has just shown me your letter to Marjory, which has greatly shocked and grieved me. As I know that the person who misled you about Marjory and Mr O'Reilly, between whom there has never been a shadow of a flirtation, is Mr Hamlin, I feel bound to tell you, not only that to my knowledge Marjory has not seen Mr O'Reilly except once since your departure; but also, as having been present on the occasion of the supposed flirtation, that Mr Hamlin imagined the flirtation, and wrote to you about it merely because he was in an ill temper, and because Marjory had annoyed him that evening by detecting a fraud in the spiritualistic *séance* in which we were engaged. Mr Hamlin has himself just told me that he does not any longer believe in the flirtation, and had no notion of creating any mischief. So, as he is not writing to you himself, I feel bound to tell you the real state of affairs, and I trust you will immediately let Marjory know that your suspicions were groundless, as she is very unhappy, and indignant with your letter.—Believe me, dear Mr Collett, yours sincerely, ANNE BROWN."

Anne stopped several times in course of writing, and read and re-read her letter. Hamlin had refused to make amends; well, she must make them for him: the matter was simple, and it was Anne's character, whenever she saw the right course, to take it without hesitation, however painful to her. Like many very honest and firm people, she had something destructive in her temper; she could, as Sacha Elaguine had said, sacrifice herself and others with a sort of sullen savage satisfaction. It was a humiliation for Hamlin, but he had deserved it; it was a bitter humiliation for herself, but her debt of gratitude towards Hamlin forced her to take the consequences of the bad that was in him as well as the good. To admit that Hamlin had, from mere womanish ill-temper, calumniated a friend, wantonly and thoughtlessly made two loving natures mistrust each other, and that he had then refused to repair the mischief of his own making,—this was intolerably bitter to Anne; still it had to be done. She put the letter on the hall table, and bade the servant post it without delay. Then she felt the full ignominy of the matter; and her whole nature recoiled from Hamlin's. Nay, it did not recoil; there was no reality to shrink from. Anne no longer felt horror as she had done when he had given her that poem about Cold Fremley; she recognised that his fault was negative, that his moral evil was moral nullity—the utter incapacity in this man, who had acted so chivalrously towards her, of perceiving when he was doing a mean thing. And the thought that she would be chained for ever to the side of a man whose whole nature was merely æsthetic, who was wholly without moral nerves or moral muscles, filled her with despair.

The next day, Hamlin sent word that he had to go and see some pictures at Oxford, and would be away for two days. Anne felt a vague hope that he was ashamed of himself. Madame Elaguine called, and with her came Cosmo Chough. The conversation, to Miss Brown's annoyance, turned upon the spiritualistic *séance* of the previous week.

"What a fool Walter is!" exclaimed Sacha. "Fancy his moping in a corner because the spirits crowned him with paper laurels! I can't understand a man not having more brass, not putting a better face on things. But Walter is a curious creature: in many respects he is not a man but a child. He has seen a great deal of life, and yet in many things he is like a girl of fifteen."

"Mr Hamlin," said Anne, evasively, "has an essentially artistic nature; the realities of the world don't appeal much to him."

"Unless an artist feel the realities of the world," said Madame Elaguine, eating some of the petals of the roses that were at her elbow, "his art will be very thin. Life must stain the artist with its colours, or his art will be tintless."

Anne had often said those same words to herself; yet somehow she knew that in Sacha Elaguine's mouth they had a different meaning; and she felt it, when, with her curious, half–childlike, and yet infinitely conscious smile, she turned to Chough.

"Don't you think so, Signor Cosmo?"

Cosmo Chough pretended that he understood, as he always did, whenever he thought that passion and the Eternal Feminine were in question; he tightened his black moustachioed lips into a long grimace, and bowed in deferential agreement.

"Of course," said the little man, sticking his single eye–glass in his eye, "we all know that our friend Hamlin will never get out of life all that perfume, that narcotic and bitter–sweet fiavour, which some other men taste, to be poisoned for ever, with their first mouthful of honey. Hamlin is, in some respects, a little more and a little less than a man."

"A goose, in short," laughed Sacha.

"He is, purely and simply, an artist. Passions, senses, all the things which belong to other men's personality, belong to him only as factors of his art. And this is perhaps not to be regretted, but to be rejoiced in. There is terrible danger of the artist being swallowed up by the man. Of the poets whom God sends on earth, two–thirds are lost to mankind: their passions, which should be merely so many means of communication between their soul and the universe, eat them up; or rather they feed themselves on what should become the world's honey. And even of those who are not lost entirely, how many are there not whose lives are engulfed by passions; to whom, alas! what they sing is but the wretched shadow of what they feel!" And Chough sighed, and fixed his eyes on his lacquered boot-tips, as much as to intimate that he, who lived on mutton-chops and spent his life nursing an epileptic wife, was of that Caliph Vathek kind.

Madame Elaguine laughed; but Chough thought it was at Hamlin, and frowned.

"Herein lies Hamlin's advantage; he is the pure artist. And, mark me," he said, looking fiercely around him, "he is none the worse for that. No, rather the better. I know no man to compare with Hamlin as a mere person; to compare with him not merely in genius, but in kindliness of temper, in purity of soul, in delicacy of thoughts. He is not merely a great artist, but a work of art; he is like a picture of Sir Galahad vivified, or like a sonnet of Dante turned into flesh—and I think Miss Brown will agree with me."

"Mr Hamlin," said Anne, slowly, "is a very generous man and a very chivalric man, and," she added, feeling as if Madame Elaguine were looking into her soul, and as if she must read ingratitude written in it, "I feel that I am indebted to him not merely for all he has done for me, but for the way in which he has done it—"

"Oh no, no!" exclaimed the polite little poet, to whom Anne was quite the goddess, "don't say that, Miss Brown; you can never owe anything to any one. Whatever a man can do, is a tribute which his nature forces him to lay down at your shrine."

"Yes," mused Madame Elaguine, following out the pattern of the carpet with her parasol "indebted—that is how one must feel towards Walter—indebted for the pleasure, &c., &c., of so charming an acquaintance; but love—one can't love where there is only artistic instinct to meet one—"

"I know nothing about such matters," said Anne, quietly.

"But, perhaps—Hamlin may be a sort of child of genius, and the man, the man who feels may come later," finished the Russian.

"When people don't feel, they don't feel," said Anne, sternly; "I mean—morally."

"By the way," exclaimed Chough, "I am reading such a delightful book—have you ever read it, Madame Elaguine?—The Letters of Mademoiselle Aïssé—"

"Who was Mademoiselle Aïssé?" asked Anne absently, forgetting that experience had taught her that it was safer not to inquire too curiously into Mr Chough's heroines.

"I suppose she was some improper lady or other—all your poetic ladies were, weren't they?" asked Madame Elaguine. "Something like your Belle Heaulmière, whom you insisted on talking about at poor Lady Brady's party, although I kept making signs to you the whole time."

"Improper?" exclaimed Chough. "Mademoiselle Aïssé was the soul of virtue—the purest woman—of the eighteenth century."

"Tell us about this purest woman of—the eighteenth century," laughed Sacha.

"She was the daughter of kings; her name was originally Ayesha, like the wife of the Prophet—but she became a slave, and was sold as a child to M. de Ferréol—I think that was his name—who was ambassador at Constantinople. M. de Ferréol sent her to his sister-in-law in Paris to educate. Aïssé grew up the most refined and accomplished woman,—you should read her letters—perfect gems!—and marvellously beautiful. Life was just opening to her, and love also, when M. de Ferréol returned from Constantinople, and said to this exquisite, proud, and pure-minded creature: 'You are my slave; I bought you, I educated you; now love me.'"

Chough paused and looked round him to watch the effect of his eloquence. But his eyes fell upon Anne. She was very white.

"Well—and what did Aïssé answer?" asked Madame Elaguine.

"Aïssé answered—let me see, what did Aïssé answer?—oh, I should spoil your pleasure were I to tell it you. I will bring you the book, dear Madame Elaguine, and you shall tell me what you think of it."

Anne felt that she had betrayed herself. To Sacha, she hoped, she believed not—but to Chough. The little poet, in his trumpery way, was really attached to Anne, whom he considered as his guardian angel; and perhaps his affection had made him understand.

"What became of Mademoiselle Aïssé?" asked Anne, some time later, as she stood by the piano where Chough was playing.

Chough looked up. "Oh—why—she—in short—afterwards—she died."

"Would you like to see the book?" asked Madame Elaguine; "I have some others on hand at present. Mr Chough shall send it to you—"

"Oh no, thank you," answered Anne, "I have a heap of books to get through; and—I don't care what happened to Mademoiselle Aïssé."

"You are very hard–hearted, Anne."

"She would not have objected to M. de Ferréol if she had remained a mere little Turkish slave–girl; she would have thought him a sort of God. She had no business to let her education make her squeamish."

"A nasty old ambassador!" said Madame Elaguine. "*I* think it was awfully hard upon her, poor thing! And was she in love with some one else, Mr Chough?"

CHAPTER IV.

WHEN Chough first told her the story of Mademoiselle Aïssé, it was as if Anne had been suddenly confronted by her own wraith, surrounded by strange and tragic lights; and the shock was very violent. But Miss Brown was too honest not to see after a minute that between her and Aïssé there was an unfathomable difference. M. de Ferréol was a mere experimentalising old *roué*, who had had a mistress prepared as he might have had a goose fattened; and what he claimed of Aïssé was her infamy. Anne's conscience smote her; she was very ungrateful. And she thought over all those scenes at the Villa Arnolfini, at Florence, nay, here in England not so long ago; she thought of Hamlin's generosity and delicacy of mind—of the quixotic way in which he had bound himself while leaving her free—of the chivalrous way in which he had dowered her, making her feel almost as if all this money, which placed her on his own level, was her own inheritance, and not his charity. She remembered all the respect, which was more of a brother than of a lover, with which he treated her—the constant manner in which he hid all her obligations to him, never letting any taunt or harsh word of hers get the better of his resolution that Anne should feel that she owed nothing to him, and that he craved for her love as he might have done for that of a queen. And it came home to her how pure, nay, how poetically and romantically noble was the love which he asked for; and she felt almost wicked when she reflected that what he wanted was to make her into the very highest thing which a man can make a woman—a sort of Beatrice, a creature to love whom will be spiritual redemption. All these things did Anne say to herself; but it cost her an effort, and the strain could not be kept up. The fact was that she had, in her terror of being unjust, refused to listen to her own plea. But it came back to her like an overwhelming flood. She could not love Hamlin; her soul recoiled from contact with his as her body might have recoiled from the forced embrace of a corpse: such a union, it seemed, would mean the death of her own nature. To be Hamlin's wife, to spend all her life by his side, hopelessly watching his growing callousness to everything for which she felt born,—to feel one generous impulse after another gradually waxing feebler, one energy after another for good becoming paralysed by the deathly moral chill of his utter heartlessness,—was this not much worse than any mere dishonour of the body, this prostitution of the spirit? Aïssé's soul at least was free; her Ferréol could not deprive her of her moral freedom, her aspirations, her powers of self-sacrifice; but with her, Anne Brown, it was different. And she repeated to herself with bitterness the warning words which Richard Brown had spoken in vain so long, long ago: "You will be his to do what he chooses; worse than his slave, his mere chattel and plaything." How little Dick had guessed the much more terrible meaning which these words would come to have for her!

Unconsciously Anne's mind reverted to the business of Marjory and Harry Collett; and her mind's eye rested for a moment upon those two lovers, to each of whom, through whatsoever of discrepancy there might be, the other represented his or her highest ideal, that other's opinion his or her highest conscience; not passionately in love, like Othello and Desdemona, or Romeo and Juliet, but persuaded to their inmost soul that in living by each other's side, and sympathising with and helping in the other's work, each would be fulfilling his or her best destiny in the world. Another woman situated like Anne might have let herself be tempted into cynicism by unconscious envy; but this was not within

Miss Brown's honest, and open-eyed, and stern nature. She never once said to herself—"Marjory and Harry will awake one day from their dream." She had dreamed, alas! and had awakened; but she recognised that these two were broad awake, and that their happiness was a reality. Anne looked at these two lovers for a moment, but without any envy or bitterness. It never even entered her mind to covet their happiness, to imagine that she might have a right to anything similar. Anne, though leaning towards socialism in her theories, was not in the least a communistic mind; she did not ask, "Why should I not get the same advantages as my neighbours?" She envied no one the prize in the lottery; she begged only for a chance. To be the wife of a man whom she loved, and who loved her—to be the companion and helpmate of some one who was striving after her own ideals; such hankerings had never passed through her mind—or, if they had, they had long since been banished. What Anne longed for, what her soul hungered after, was merely negative freedom. Freedom to sympathise and to aspire—to do whatever little she still might to carve herself out a spiritual life of her own, no matter how mean and insignificant; freedom to live in that portion of her which was most worthy of life. To gain her bread, no matter how harshly; to be of some use, to teach at a school or nurse at a hospital; nay, to be able merely to encourage others to do what she might not,—this was all that Anne asked; and this, in her future as the wife of Hamlin, as the queen of this æsthetic world, which seemed to poison and paralyse her soul, was what she knew she could not have, what she knew she must do without.

"I am a selfish brute," she suddenly said to herself, "wasting the time which is still mine,"—and she took down her books of political economy, and tried to fix her attention upon them, and think out a scheme of the lessons and exercises which she would give to the shop-girls at the Working Women's Club. But what was the use of doing this? Hamlin, she knew, loathed the notion of her teaching at the Club; he would never let her teach there; and, once his wife, she understood him sufficiently to be fully aware that he would consider himself completely empowered to make her do or leave alone whatever he chose.

Still Anne tried to work on courageously. In the afternoon she went to hear one of Professor Richmond's lectures. This was the fervent young positivist whom Cousin Dick so much admired, and whose intense moral convictions had done a good deal to keep Anne out of the slough of desponding pessimism round which she had been some time hovering. Andrew Richmond was a man who had many slanderers, many of whom he has now left behind him—their misrepresentations having been more long-lived than he; for he had passed through many phases of thought, and, being perfectly honest, he had never been able to become unjust to any, and thus had made enemies not merely among the men whose beliefs he had abandoned, but among those also whose beliefs he had accepted without accepting their follies. He stood very alone; and it was perhaps this isolation—this obvious indifference of the man to all save his own reason and conscience—which added to the solemnity of his convictions; and made him appear, more than any one else, in the light of a priest of morality, of a prophet of the advent of justice. Anne had never spoken to Richmond; but she felt that, of all human souls, this one did the most to keep up the courage of her own. This was one of the last discourses which the poor dying positivist ever delivered; and it was the more earnest for the sense of his approaching end. He spoke this time, or, as his ridiculers called it, he preached upon the relation of duty to progress; upon the value of each good impulse carried out, and each evil one resisted, in making morality more natural and spontaneous in the world; and he insisted especially upon the danger, to people whose ideas of right and wrong rested no longer upon any priestly authority, of the individual sophisticating himself into the belief that in yielding to the preferences of his own nature he was following the highest law, and that any special usefulness ought legitimately to be bought at the expense of departing from the moral rules of the world.

"The danger of our epoch of moral transition," he said, "lies in the temptation of the individual to say to himself—'If I am willing to sacrifice myself, have I not a right also to sacrifice the established opinions of others?'"

"I detest that man Richmond," Madame Elaguine had once said; "he puts an end to all self-sacrifice."

"If you mean the sacrifice of one's peace of mind and social dignity to the passion of another person and to one's own, he certainly does," Richard Brown had answered sternly.

At the door of the lecture-room Anne met her cousin.

"Are you driving to Hammersmith?" he asked.

"No; I am going to walk."

Anne had made it a rule for the last two or three months to deprive herself of all luxuries. She did not wish to enjoy everything that she had a right to; she had also a stern pleasure in doing the things most repugnant to her; and a walk through the London streets, in murky spring weather, was to Anne's Italian temper, nurtured with æsthetic delicacy, one of the most disagreeable of expeditions.

"But it is drizzling and horribly muddy," said Richard Brown, looking at her as he buttoned her ulster over her massive figure. "Surely Hamlin will be very much shocked if you come into the house with mud on your shoes? But if you are really going to walk I will accompany you, if you don't mind, because I'm going in that direction."

"Where are you going?"

"To Hammersmith; I have some business there." And Brown looked once more at his cousin as he opened his umbrella over her.

"Will you take my arm, Anne?" Richard Brown was not a lady's man, and there was something awkward and unaccustomed in his request.

"I am big enough to take care of myself, I think, Dick. And I know you hate having women to drag along; I have watched you going into dinner-parties often enough."

"It is out of my line, you're right."

For some time they walked along in silence through the black oozy streets, crammed with barrows of fruit, round which gathered the draggled dripping women, their babies huddled up in their torn shawls, their hair untidy and dank beneath their once lilac or pale-pink smut-engrained bonnets; the cabs, shining blue-black, ploughed through the mud; the heavy drays splashed from gutter to gutter; the houses were black and oozy; the very raindrops on the railings looked black; the sky was a dirty dull-grey waste; only the scarlet letter-boxes stood out coloured in the general smutty, foggy, neutral tint.

"Do you remark that public-houses are the only places which make an attempt at architecture and ornament?" said Dick grimly, as they passed the ground-glass windows and colonnade and coloured glass globes of one of these establishments. "Did it not strike you, Italian as you are, that in this country, which has invented high art, the only things called palaces, except those inhabited by royalty, are pot-houses? Why do your æsthetic friends keep all their æstheticism for indoors? Why don't they build themselves houses which will be some pleasure to the poor people who pass?"

Always that indirect attack upon Hamlin and his friends: it was just and reasonable; yet, coming from Brown, it somehow grated upon Anne.

"That will come later," she said. "The first thing is that the upper classes become accustomed to beautiful things. You can't expect them to mind hideous outsides to their houses if they are indifferent to hideous insides. I don't think," she added boldly, "that æstheticism has had much generosity of aspiration in it so far, except in isolated men like Ruskin and Morris; but I am sure it will eventually improve some matters even for the lower classes."

"Nero rebuilt Rome, didn't he," sneered Brown, "after he had amused himself burning it down?"

They fell to talking about the lecture, and then about Richard Brown's plans.

"I hope to get into Parliament next elections," he said, "and then I shall retire from Mr Gillespie's firm."

"Why? They say you can make a big fortune if you keep on."

"I have quite money enough; I am a rich man. You wouldn't have thought that possible, would you, Nan, two or three years ago? Almost as rich as Hamlin, do you know, young woman?" and he turned and looked at her. There was a curious expression, what she could not understand, except that it was defiant, in Dick's face.

"I am glad to hear it. It is a fine thing to have money; it enables one to do generous things—like what Mr Hamlin did for me, for instance." Anne could not have explained why she felt bound, at this particular moment, to throw Hamlin's generosity in her cousin's face.

"Ah, well," answered Brown, suppressing something he had been about to retort, "of course I could not formerly have done what he did for you; but I would have gladly spent every shilling I had, Anne, to educate you, so that your father might have been proud of you."

"I know you would, Dick—you are very kind." And yet, thought Anne, until he had been piqued by Hamlin's offer, he had forgotten all about her. "But why do you intend to leave your business?"

"Because I want to give myself up entirely to studying social questions, and my business would suffer if I gave it only partial attention."

And he proceeded to explain the various questions which he intended studying, the various evils into whose reason he wished to look.

"Reform has been too much the leisure-time amusement of men," he said. "People have thought that it requires less training to touch, nay, to sound, social wounds, than to set a broken arm or dress a wound. We must find the scientific basis for our art. And it is a very, very long art, and life is very, very short. For my part, I feel that my knowledge is to what it should be what the knowledge you may get out of a school primer of physiology is to the knowledge required by a great surgeon. I don't suppose I or any of my generation will succeed in doing much practical good; but we shall have made the public ready for certain views on our subjects, and rendered it easier for our practical followers to get their education. There is nothing very glorious to be done at present: no giving out of brilliant new ideas or making of successful revolutions; only patient grubbing at facts and patient working on the public mind."

"Is that enough for an ambitious man?"

"One must pocket one's ambition. What we want is knowledge, not conspicuous personalities."

Anne was silent. Dick's words were like military music to her. Oh to be able to join him, to march by his side, to carry his arms!

"Go on Dick, please. It does one good to hear of these things."

Dick went on.

"You must not overwork yourself," said Anne, anxiously. "Just think if you were to break down, as so many men have done—as poor Richmond is doing."

"Oh, I am strong. The only thing which concerns me is my sight. I find I am already unable to read of an evening. There's no danger of blindness, but the doctor says I must not work by candle–light. Oh, there's no mischief. I shall engage a secretary. I know plenty of young men who would come, even for a small salary. There is the son of one of our head workmen, a very intelligent lad, of whom I am thinking; but perhaps he is not sufficiently educated yet. I must have some one who knows German and French, and so forth."

Anne felt a lump in her throat. Oh that she had been a man, instead of being this useless, base creature of mere comely looks, a woman, set apart for the contemplation of æsthetes! If she had been a man, and could have helped a man like Richard Brown!

"But I am not certain of my plans just yet," added Brown, and he dropped the subject. They walked on for some moments in silence; then he began questioning her about Lewis, and Chough, and Dennistoun.

"Chough is a dear good little man," said Anne; "he is very absurd and vain, and fond of talking and writing about wicked things, which I am sure he doesn't understand any more than I. But he is so self–sacrificing, and warm–hearted, and true. Dennistoun, poor creature, is very morbid and faddy, and, I think, hates me; but I am very sorry for him. As to Lewis, he may be a very good man, but I don't like him—"

"I suppose you have heard what people say,—that Mr Lewis had rather a bad influence upon Hamlin some years ago—in short, made him take to eating opium, or haschisch, or something similar?"

"No—I had never heard that," and Anne seemed suddenly to understand her instinctive horror of Lewis.

"Does Hamlin see much of him now?"

"A great deal—more than I can at all sympathise with. Lewis is rather a sore subject between us; he knows I don't like him, and yet he is very fond of him."

"I suppose Lewis flatters him very much."

"I suppose so."

Anne resented being thus cross-questioned about Hamlin, but she was quite unable to prevaricate in her answers—her nature was too frank, and Richard's questions were too direct.

"You are not very happy with Mr Hamlin," he suddenly asked, or rather affirmed.

Anne flushed, but did not answer at once. "I have an unlucky temper," she said, after a moment. "I am too exacting with people. I can't get out of my own individuality sufficiently, I fear."

Richard looked at her with pity, and at the same time with that implacable scrutiny of his.

"You feel your nature narrowed by all this æsthetic world around you," he said. "You find these men selfish, mean, weak, shallow—"

"Chough is not selfish. As to Dennistoun and Lewis, I told you I disliked them."

"You are equivocating, Anne. You know I am not speaking of Dennistoun, or Lewis, or Chough. You find that Hamlin drags you down, freezes all your best aspirations."

Anne turned very white and trembled.

"Mr Hamlin is a poet, an artist; he is not a philanthropist or a thinker. But he has done for me more than I believe any man has ever done for any woman."

"But—you don't love him?"

Richard had stopped as they walked along the Hammersmith embankment. It was a very quiet spot, and not a soul was out in the thin, grey, drizzly fog.

Anne hesitated for a moment.

"I feel very much attached to Mr Hamlin on account of his generosity towards me—and I feel I can never repay it." She did not look in Brown's face as she answered, but stared vaguely at the river, at the dripping trees, the grey willow branches pulled backwards and forwards by the grey current; at the houses opposite, and the boats dim in the fog.

"You don't love him?" repeated Richard in a whisper. "Anne, answer me."

"I don't see what right you have to ask me such a question, Richard."

"No? Well, I do—and you shall see why. You are not his wife; why should you try and tell lies? Do you or do you not love Hamlin, Anne?"

Anne looked for a moment at the swirling waters, at the willow twigs whirled hither and thither.

"I suppose I do not."

There was a pause.

"You do not love him, and you still contemplate marrying him?"

"I contemplate nothing at all. Mr Hamlin has not yet asked me to marry him, and perhaps he never may."

"Nonsense, Anne. And when he does ask you, what will you answer?"

"I shall answer Yes. I am bound to do it. Mr Hamlin has done all, all for me. If he wish to marry me, I cannot refuse him the only thing which I can give in return for his generosity."

Richard Brown burst into a strange shrill laugh.

"The only thing which you can give in return for his generosity!" he exclaimed, but always in the same undertone. "Who first made use of those words, Nan? The only thing which you can give in return for his generosity! Did not some one use those very words to you, long, long ago in Florence, when Mr Hamlin first proposed to educate you, and your cousin said that you were running the risk of selling yourself? But, by God! you shall not sell yourself, Anne. Do you know what you are giving him in return for what you call his generosity?—that is to say, in return for the whim which made him educate a beautiful woman, that he might show her off and have a beautiful wife, if he chose. Do you know what it is? Your love, eh? You have none to give; you have said so yourself. Your body? your honour? Nay, every prostitute, every kitchen slut can give him that. And I suppose such things do not exist for a delicately nurtured lady, a ward of Mr Walter Hamlin's. No; you are giving him your soul, selling it to him, prostituting it as any common woman would prostitute her body."

"Richard," said Anne, hotly, "you are my cousin, and have been very good to me, but that gives you no right to insult me."

"My words are ugly; and what are the things which you would do? Anne, you shall listen to me," and he laid his hand heavily on her arm.

"You can make me stand here," she answered icily, "but you cannot make me listen."

"I *can* make you listen. Oh, Anne," and his voice became suddenly supplicating, "do not be womanish, and refuse to listen because I speak disagreeable things. Answer me, on your honour: have I a right to let you sacrifice your happiness, your honour, your usefulness in the world, to let you defile and ruin all these, by becoming what is equivalent to a mere legalised mistress—the wife of a man whom you despise? You have a debt towards Hamlin: I grant it, though you must be well aware how little real generosity there was in his choice of you; but you have a debt also towards yourself. You have no right to pay for Hamlin's kindness by the falsehood, the degradation, of marrying a man whom you do not love, by the sacrifice of all the nobler part of your nature which that man will crush out in you."

"If there is anything noble in me, Dick, no one can ever crush it out; and I do not see what real degradation there will be in honestly carrying out my part of a bargain which has been honestly carried out towards me."

Richard paused for a minute.

"But," he cried, "you mistake, Anne; you forget what that bargain was."

"No, I do not. Mr Hamlin promised to marry me whenever I should ask him to do so, and—"

"And he left you free, perfectly free to marry him or not as you pleased!"

"*He* left me free; and it is just that generosity of his, in binding himself, and not me, which obliges me, if he wants me, to say Yes."

"That is an absurd quibble, Anne. If Hamlin's leaving you free bound you all the more, why, then, he did not leave you free, and you need not be bound by a piece of magnanimity which never existed."

"On the contrary, *you* are quibbling, Dick. You know very well that Mr Hamlin meant to leave me free; and it is for this intention that I am, more than for anything else, grateful."

Richard turned round.

"Fool that I am!" he cried, "to believe in you and not see through your woman's tergiversation! You say you do not love Hamlin, but you do; you may despise him, feel his emptiness—I grant it all—be dissatisfied with him. Oh, I know it! But you love him all the same, and you would not for the world give him up, even if he asked you to."

Anne laughed bitterly. "The usual generalisations about women. Because I will not do a dishonourable thing, I must needs be a self-deluding fool. No; I do *not* love Hamlin. I love him no more than this!" And Anne broke a twig off a bush and threw it into the stream.

"You do not? Then, if Hamlin were to release you,—if he were to say, 'I want to marry some one else,'—would you—would you not regret him, his poetry, his good looks, his fame, his fortune?"

"It would be the happiest day of my life!" cried poor Anne, despairingly.

"Then that day must come. Anne, I cannot see you sacrificed. I cannot see you lost to yourself and to the world. You *must* not marry Hamlin. I will provide for you; I will take care of you. You shall help me in my work!"

"Poor Dick!" said Anne gently, touched by this enthusiasm, "you are very good; but I fear—I fear I shall never have any need of your help; and I would never burden another man—never have a debt again—if I were remitted this one."

"You would have no debt," cried Brown. "Anne, I am not a woman's man. I don't know how to say such things. But ever since I have got really to know you, I have felt if only I could have such a woman as that always by my side—to tell her all my plans, and be helped in all my work . . ."

Richard looked straight before him: Anne could see his face quiver. A coldness came all over her: a coldness and a heat. She felt as if she must cry out. It was too sudden, too wonderful. The vision of being Richard Brown's wife overcame her like some celestial vision a fasting saint. But she made an effort over herself. "I am bound, bound," she said; "but if ever I be released . . . "

She hesitated: the longing for what she knew herself to be renouncing was too great.

"Anne," cried Richard, seizing her hand, "I love you—I love you—I want you—I must have you!"

It was like the outburst of another nature, a strange, unsuspected ego, bursting out from beneath the philanthropist's cool and self-sacrificing surface.

That sudden contact gave Anne a shock which woke her, restored her to herself; it horrified her almost. She made him let go her hand.

"If ever I be released," she said, "I will remain free. I do not love you, Dick."

She was sorry the moment after she had said it.

"I have gone too far," cried Richard.

"Good-bye," said Anne. "We have been talking too long—and—you won't resume the subject, will you?"

There was a command, a threat implied in her voice. Brown somehow felt ashamed of himself.

"Not since you wish it," he said flatly.

"Good-bye," said Anne. And she walked away and entered the house—Hamlin's house.

CHAPTER V.

THE sudden revelation of her cousin's feeling was more than a shock, it was a blow to Anne. In her loneliness, in her dreary waiting for the hour of sacrifice, Richard Brown's friendship had, almost without her knowing it, been her great consolation and support. It had given her a sense of safety and repose to think that, in the midst of all the morbid passion and fantastic vanity which seemed to surround her, there was a possibility of honest companionship, of affection which meant merely reciprocal esteem and sympathy in the objects of life; wholesome prose in the middle of unhealthy poetry. This was now gone: Richard Brown loved her, wanted her; it was the old nauseous story over again; the sympathy, the comradeship, the quiet brotherly and sisterly affection had all been a sham, a sham for her and for himself. Was Mrs Macgregor right, and was there, of really genuine and vital in the world, only the desire of the man for the woman and of the woman for the man, with all its brood of vanity and baseness, and all its trappings of poetry and sympathy and self-sacrifice? Anne looked round her, and she saw men like Chough and Dennistoun and Lewis, base or doing their best to become it; Hamlin, her girlish ideal of poetical love, had gone the same way; and now the one man who had remained to her as an object of friendship and respect, her cousin Dick, had preached against selfish æstheticism, had talked her into his positivistic philanthropy—had conjured her to respect her nobler nature, her soul, her generous instincts—had supplicated her not to degrade herself,—nay, had quibbled with right and wrong, had urged her to break her trust,—what for? that he might satisfy his whim of possessing her. The solitude and the chilliness around Anne had increased; she wished for good, but she disbelieved in its existence. Add to this that she felt she was now no longer at liberty to see so much of Dick as she had formerly done; instead of a consolation and a support, his presence seemed to her now more of a danger and an insult. So she waited, hopeless and solitary, for the hour of the sacrifice to strike; for Hamlin to claim her. To fulfil that debt, to suffer that moral death–blow, seemed to her now the one certainty, the one aim of her life.

Such was the bulk of Miss Brown's condition; but there were streakings of another colour which made it, on the whole, only more gloomy. The possibility, the vision which had for a moment been projected on to her mind, of becoming Richard Brown's wife, of sharing in all those thoughts and endeavours which were her highest ideal, would return to her every now and then in strange sudden gleams. And this possibility, or rather this which was an impossibility, made the real necessity of her life only the gloomier for the contrast. Anne had vaguely aspired after a life of nobler sympathies and stronger aims, but she had never gone so far as to dream of sharing the life of her cousin; and she thought that, had matters been different, had she been free, had Hamlin not claimed her, had Richard not loved her (for his love, his selfish tempting her away from her duty, seemed to her a sort of dishonour to him and her), she would have had the fulfilment of her most far–fetched desires within her grasp,—merely increased moral numbness, the sullen pain of resignation, towards a fate which was too slow in coming.

Anne did not pay much heed to Hamlin and his doings: it seemed to her, whose life in the last months had appeared like years, that it was always the same monotony; Hamlin was waiting for her to fall in love with him, watching whether she was not in love already; offering her, in those vague, Platonic, elegiac speeches of his about the necessity of a higher life of which he no longer had much hope, of a pure passion which he feared he was unworthy to experience, an opportunity for saying "I will teach you how to love." Veiled in Dantesque mysticism, muffled in Shakespearian obscurity, such was, to her who understood and was expected to understand, the gist of all the poems which he wrote. The day would come, Anne saw it clearly, when some trifling quarrel, some trifling jealousy, some rebuff to his vanity, or some sense of more than usual vacuity, would get the better of Hamlin's patience, and when he would say to Anne that he loved her and that her love was his life. She had gone over it all so often in fancy, with the bitter sarcasm of understanding that whole, to her so tragic, little comedy. But had she been a person more observant and penetrating than she was (for her long delusion about her cousin Richard plainly shows that she was neither), or had she been less engrossed in her own conception of events, Miss Brown might have noticed, as spring turned into summer, that certain slight changes were taking place in Hamlin. He had, without any intentional rupture, taken to seeing much less of Chough and Dennistoun; he scarcely ever visited his old master, Mrs Spencer, or any others of the school; he refused invitations to parties, or if he had accepted, found them too great a bore at the last moment; the only house, except that at Hammersmith, which he frequented, was Madame Elaguine's. He used to attend all her spiritualistic *séances*, and alternate between finding spiritualism a vulgar fraud and a mystic possibility; he used to quarrel with Edmund Lewis, and at the same time to seek his company more than any other man's. He would vacillate also between the most extreme opinions about his cousin Sacha. One day he would entertain Anne by the hour about her virtues, her talents, her persecution; the next he would be captiously fault-finding, accusing Madame Elaguine of being a brainless little flirt, a mere ordinary Russian, who cared only for excitement and being perpetually *en scène*.

"What is the use of asking people to be intense when it is not their nature?" Anne would ask, not without bitterness in her own heart. "If you find a pleasant friend, be satisfied and thankful for your good luck."

Be it as it may, Hamlin was restless, subject to strange ups and downs of humour, sometimes in a state of vague unaccountable cheerfulness, sometimes horribly depressed. To any one but Anne it would have occurred that there must be some novelty in his life. But Anne did not see; indeed, from a sort of instinct, she observed Hamlin as little as possible: she had loved him when she had not known him; the less she saw, except his gentle, chivalric, poetic, idealising surface, the better.

But one day—it might be a fortnight after the memorable walk home from Richmond's lecture—Anne found among her letters one, evidently delivered by hand or dropped into the letter- box, the address upon which. puzzled her considerably. It was not merely that the handwriting was unknown to her, but that it was so utterly unlike any human handwriting that could be conceived; it was like a child's elaborate copy of print, but executed with a precision, and at the same time a certain artistic *chic*, of which a child is incapable. Had she been in Italy, Anne would have expected to find within that envelope one of those marvellously written out and illuminated sonnets which certain needy individuals, counts and marquises fallen into bad circumstances and anxious to redeem their only bed from the pawnbroker's, serve up at regular intervals to English and Americans, "the many illustrious qualities of whose mind and heart, as well known as their noble family," are supposed to include munificence to beggars. To Anne's astonishment the letter which she found actually was in Italian. But it was Italian of Stratford-atte-Bow, and her first impulse was to burst out laughing. But the next moment she reddened with surprise and indignation.

"*MADONNA MIA*," began this epistle, which had evidently been concocted with a 'Decameron' and a Baedeker's travelling phrase-book, and which sounded like English written by a German waiter who should have taken to Spenser after the first dozen lessons,—"Inasmuch as it always is the duty of the honest to warn the unsuspecting, and the most honourable are always those who suspect least, your true friend and well-wisher desires you may keep an eye upon the machinations of a base woman; and be on your guard against the friendship [underlined] of cousins."

Anne turned the note round and round, and read and re-read it, her heart beating as if she had received a slap in the face. "The *friendship* of cousins." Her first thought was that this was an allusion to herself and Richard Brown; some one had understood what she had not, and was suspecting what was not true. But then her mind picked up that other mysterious phrase, "the machinations of a base woman." The cousins were not herself and Dick, but Hamlin and Sacha Elaguine, and that was the base woman alluded to. It was as if a great light had shone in Anne's face; she was dazzled, dazed. The friendship of two cousins! Was there, then, more than friendship between them? Did Hamlin love Sacha, or Sacha Hamlin? Anne gave a great sigh; but it was a sigh of relief,—the sigh of the drowning wretch who is dragged on shore—the sigh of the hunted fugitive who sees his pursuers turn back. The friendship of cousins? Why, then, she was saved, she was free! But her excitement lasted only a minute. Was she to believe an anonymous letter, evidently malicious, evidently intended to slander an innocent woman, to sow discord or to ruin her own happiness? It was evidently from an enemy of Madame Elaguine's; it could not be from a friend of her own; for a friend would have spoken to her clearly and openly, or would have spared her what, in the eyes of the world, which regarded her as Hamlin's affianced bride, must have been a horrible revelation. It was an infamous or ridiculous calumny. From whom did it come? Anne thought for a long time; she counted up her own enemies and Madame Elaguine's. At one moment she suspected Edmund Lewis, at another Mrs Spencer; but she was too honest to credit any one of them with such a piece of treachery. Madame Elaguine's mysterious enemies—yes, it must be they! thought Anne; it must be a new trick of theirs, a device for alienating her from her new friends. Anne's heart sank. Why must such terrible temptations be put upon her?

Miss Brown meditated for some time upon what she ought to do. She felt indignant with the mysterious author of the letter; and she felt that, as it contained a slander, it was her duty to let those whom it accused know the whole matter. Should she show that paper to Hamlin? Once in her life, Anne gave way to a movement of cowardice. That letter, shown by her to Hamlin, would, she knew, bring the catastrophe. Hamlin would be furious and delighted; he would think she was jealous and unhappy; he would on the spot declare that he loved her, and ask her to be his wife. This consummation of her sacrifice, which, in the dull apathy of the last fortnight, she had almost prayed for, now terrified her. When it came, she was ready; but to hasten it—to bring it down untimely on herself—to do that, Anne had not the heart. After all, it concerned Madame Elaguine most, and she would doubtless have some clue to the writer of the letter, and consequently take the matter less to heart. Anne determined to show the letter to her. She thought she would go to her at once, or write; but a faint, faint, almost unconscious instinct of self-preservation bade her wait awhile; wait till she should have an opportunity of seeing Madame Elaguine in the natural course of events.

Miss Brown had made up her mind that the mysterious letter had no sort of truth in it; yet despite this decision, which lay, cut and dry, on the surface of her consciousness, a hidden imperceptible movement was going on within her. She seemed suddenly to remember things which she had not at the time noticed, to see things which had not before existed, and must still have been there yesterday as well as to-day. Things which had been meaningless acquired a meaning; things which had seemed without connection began to group themselves. A change had taken place of late in Hamlin; he had become solitary and morose, and more than usually up and down in spirits—he had seen only Sacha and her. How much had he seen of Sacha? Anne did not know, but she imagined a great deal. Then she remembered how he had taken to finding fault with the little woman, to running her down systematically to himself and to Anne. Could it be that he felt himself tempted to break his engagement? Anne knew Hamlin too well by this time to credit him with that. If such a thing should happen,—if, finding insensibly that Anne was not what he had imagined, disappointed with her coldness, hurt by her censoriousness, and attracted by a woman who was everything that she was not—Hamlin should ever come to feel for Sacha more than mere friendship, it was not in his nature to perceive his danger and to struggle; he would let himself go to sleep in the pleasantness of a new sensation, he would drift on vaguely, and start up in surprise.

A new love was for him the most poignant of temptations,—a new love in its still half-unconscious, Platonic, vague condition; and he was not a man to resist such a temptation; indeed he had gone through life with the philosophy that a poet may dally with any emotion, however questionable, as long as he does not actually commit a dishonourable action. Oh no, Hamlin's ups and downs could not be struggles or remorse; so Anne decided that it was all fancy, all calumny. And she determined to give the letter to Sacha on the first opportunity.

Madame Elaguine at last made up her mind that her little Helen ought to learn something; and with the impulsiveness of her nature, she determined that she, whom she had always kept under her own eyes, should go to school. Why there should be such a swing of the pendulum, and why Madame Elaguine should not rather hire a governess to teach the child in her own house, Miss Brown could not explain, except by the capriciousness, the tendency always to be in extremes, of Hamlin's cousin. Anyhow, Sacha had determined that Helen must soon go to school, and she had written to Anne begging her, before the child went, to permit her to share for a week or two the lessons which Miss Brown was giving the little Choughs. "I know," she wrote, "that my poor little child is not fit to be turned loose among other children yet; I know she is too ignorant, too sensitive, too much accustomed to life with her elders. To learn with Mr Chough's children, to play with them, will take the keen edge off; and also, I know, my dearest Anne, that if anything can make this (I fear, alas! alas! to my shame) over-sensitive and self-willed little savage more human, more desirous of being good, and of raising herself, it will be your influence. I have often felt what it would have been for me to have had a friend like you, and I feel what it will be for my child."

Anne was touched by this letter. Poor Madame Elaguine, although she did care too much for Baudelaire and Gautier, and did tell too many anecdotes about married women's lovers and married men's *cocottes* for Anne's taste, was yet a good and brave little woman; and she must be helped, if one could help her. And Anne was doubly indignant about that anonymous letter she put in her pocket, and went to call on Hamlin's cousin.

Madame Elaguine was in one of her unstrung moments. Anne found her lying on a sofa, a heap of books about her, reading none, fidgety and vacant. She brightened up for a moment on Miss Brown's entry, and received her with a kind of rapturous gratitude, quite out of all proportion; but she speedily relapsed into her depressed condition. Anne thought it better not to introduce the business at once.

"I want to know," she said, "why you are suddenly so anxious to send your little Helen to school, when you said, only a few days ago, that you could not bear even that a stranger should have any influence upon her."

Madame Elaguine hesitated. "Oh, dear Anne," she suddenly exclaimed, "I am a poor, weak, vacillating creature, always in excesses. You *must* have pity on me. I suppose it is just because I was so horribly selfish about my child that I have been crushed suddenly with the necessity of sacrificing my feelings completely. It comes home to me—and oh, you cannot think what it means to me!—that I am ruining my child, that she will turn out merely another myself—another wretched, weak, unhappy creature, with just morality enough to make her utterly miserable, and just common-sense enough to make her feel her own silliness. It is a terrible thing for a mother to say; but it is true, and I must say it: I am not fit to bring up my own child—I am not worthy to do it."

Anne looked at the Russian, who had raised herself on her sofa convulsively, and thatched and torn to pieces a flower which was lying on her, with a great look of pity.

"I am not bad!" cried Sacha—"I am not bad! I want to be good; but I can't. Oh, and I can't teach my child anything, not even the multiplication table," and she suddenly burst out laughing.

Anne did not know whether to cry or to laugh.

"I quite understand your wishing that Helen should get the habit of work, and should learn something," she said, in her business-like way; "but I cannot see the advantage of sending her to school. She is far too nervous and delicate, and far too much accustomed to indulgence, to get anything but harm from a school. Were she a mere strong, sturdy, spoilt child, it would do her an immense deal of good; but a child, you admit it yourself, so morbidly and almost physically sensitive, would only be miserable at school, and probably be terrified by unaccustomed discipline and want of sympathy. Don't you think it would be wiser to get Helen a thoroughly good governess, so that she could learn something, and yet be in your house?"

"I won't have a governess; they are all good-for-nothings. I won't have spies in the house!" exclaimed Madame Elaguine, vehemently.

"Nonsense!" said Anne; "how can you talk like that? You know that governesses are just as good as schoolmistresses; and for you and Helen such a plan would be in every way preferable."

"I won't have any one in the house to pry into my affairs!" repeated Sacha, hotly. "Helen *must* go to school."

Anne felt angry with the little woman.

"Of course it is for you to choose," she said; "but I confess I can't see why you should not have a governess any more than other people." She felt as if there were something wrong here.

"And do you forget what my life is?" cried Sacha; "do you forget that I am the daily, hourly victim of unseen enemies? Would you have me admit some one to my house, that she might play into their hands, or, at all events, pry into my misfortune?"

Anne had forgotten that. How unjust she was!

"True," she said; "I think we might find a governess who, even under your circumstances, might be safely admitted into the house. But I can understand your unconquerable aversion to the idea, so we had better look out for a school, and, till one is found, I shall be delighted if you will send Helen to me. I fear I can't do much for her, but at all events she will meet the Choughs, who are very good little girls."

Madame Elaguine rose, and, to Anne's im– measurable surprise, she flung herself on her neck, and began to sob.

"Oh Anne, dearest Anne," she said, "you are so good to me—so good, so very good—and I don't deserve it at all—indeed I know I don't."

"Nonsense; you are unwell and unstrung about Helen, and you are just making yourself miserable. Do try and be quiet, and reflect that there is nothing whatever to be miserable about."

Miss Brown, Vol. 3

Somehow or other Miss Brown, for all her good-nature, always had a harsh instinct whenever she saw Sacha in such a condition as this—an instinct that the Russian could prevent it—that such fits of tears and abjectness were mere self-indulgence, and self-indulgence which was utterly incompatible with Anne's idea of self-respect.

But Madame Elaguine could not be reined in. She fell back in an arm-chair in an agony of hysterical sobbing, mixed with ghastly laughing.

"It is not nonsense; it is true—it is true; I don't deserve it. I deserve that you should hate me. Oh Anne, you must hate me; but it is not my fault. I hate him! I have always hated him! I have told him so; but he won't believe. Oh, indeed it is not my fault. But of course you hate me, you . . ." and she suddenly burst out laughing.

Anne was very white. She had heard and she had understood; but she had no right to have heard or to have understood.

Suddenly Sacha started up and looked strangely about her.

"What! you are here?" she asked, with a start as if of terror. "Oh, what have I been talking about? Oh, I am sure I have been talking nonsense!"

"Poor little woman!" said Anne; "yes, you **have** been talking nonsense; you are afraid of having a governess for Helen, lest—"

"Ah!" cried Madame Elaguine, with a sigh of relief. "Oh, you don't know what it is to have such a fit. One feels one is talking lies, and yet that one must go on. I never had any such things before they began to persecute me. It is almost the worst part of my misfortune. Fancy seeing, feeling one's self becoming day by day more abject, and being unable to stop it. Oh, I still feel so frightened! something dreadful must have happened while I had that fit just now. Do call for some tea, Anne, darling; I feel so shaken, as if something had happened."

"You will feel all right when you have had some tea," said Anne. "Tell me, have they, have those people been frightening you of late?"

Madame Elaguine nodded. "Only last night; you don't know what happened. I didn't intend telling you—look here—but it is that that has put me into such a state," and opening the door of her bedroom, Sachs pointed to the wall opposite.

Over Madame Elaguine's bed hung a painted portrait of little Helen; but where the face should have been was a dark spot.

"Good heavens! what have they done?" cried Anne.

"Oh, they have only cut out Mademoiselle Hélène's face," said the Swiss maid, who was sitting in the room, with a shrug. "For my part, I am accustomed to such tricks, and so, I should think, must be Madame also."

Something cynical and insolent in the woman struck Anne very much.

"How horrible!" she said, leading Sacha back to the drawing-room. "I can quite understand your being excited to-day, and feeling anxious about Helen."

"It is because of that," said Sacha, with clenched teeth, "that I want to send Helen to school. She will be safer there than here. If things go on as now, I shall have to send Helen to a convent; I am no protection to her."

"You must marry, and have a husband to take care of you," said Anne, quietly.

Madame Elaguine turned scarlet. Was she afraid of having let out her secret? But to Anne's surprise, instead of looking anxious, a sudden look of triumphant amusement passed over her face, a strange brazen look, and she burst out laughing—

"Ah yes, marry!—that would be a fine idea!—and whom, pray? Perhaps Lewis or Chough. True—I forgot—he has a wife! Ah no, a rolling stone like me must always be solitary."

"You need not always be a rolling stone," said Anne, gently. "But I must go—good-bye, dear Madame Elaguine."

At the door she met Hamlin. It seemed to her that he looked guilty, and coloured.

"I have been to see your cousin; she has had another horrid trick played to her. Go up to her, it will do her good to see you; she is very lonely, poor little woman."

Hamlin was unnerved by the allusion to the persecution. He stood silent for a moment, with a long lingering look on Anne, like a man making a mental comparison.

"You are very good, Miss Brown," he said, slowly; "there is no other woman in the world like you."

"Sacha has been more tried than I," answered Anne. And Hamlin went up and Miss Brown went out.

CHAPTER VI.

MISS BROWN did not hand over the anonymous letter either to Madame Elaguine or to Hamlin. She felt that she had now no longer a right to do so. Sacha had, in the vague pouring out of words of that fit which Anne had witnessed, let out her secret; but Anne had no right to use it or to act upon it. She could only watch and wait.

Wait!—but in what a different spirit! Wait, not for the hour of death, but for the moment of freedom, of complete freedom.

"What has happened to you?" asked Mrs Spencer, meeting her on her way back from Madame Elaguine's. "Why, you look quite another being, Anne—as if some one had left you a fortune!"

"No one has left me anything," said Anne. "I feel very happy, that's all."

"But where in all this wretched London have you been that you should feel happy?"

Anne laughed.

"I have been to see Madame Elaguine."

Mrs Spencer frowned.

"Well, that wouldn't be enough to make *me* feel happy, I confess. Was Walter Hamlin there? I believe it's his safest address now, isn't it?"

"Mr Hamlin was there," answered Anne, sternly.

"Mark my words!" said Mrs Spencer that evening to her father and husband, and to one or two of those well-thinking æsthetes *de la vieille roche*, whom Hamlin had basely deserted. "Mark my words! Anne Brown has got impatient with all this philandering of Walter's about that precious Russian of his. There has been a grand scene, and Hamlin has come round to reason. I met her returning from that Elaguine woman's to-day, and she never looked so happy in her life. She said Hamlin had been there, and I know that she gave them both a bit of her mind. She's a proud woman, Anne Brown, and could squash that little Russian vixen like that!"

"But, my dear Edith," objected her father, seated among an admiring crowd in his dusty studio at Hampstead, among his ghastly Saviours on gilded grounds, and Nativities, in despite of perspective—"how de ye know that there's ever been any philandering between 'em?"

"Oh papa, really now you are too provoking!"

"Oh, Mr Saunders, how do we know anything?" chorussed the two or three elderly poetesses and untidy Giottesque painters of the circle.

"P'raps ye don't know anything, any of ye!"

Mrs Spencer sighed, as much as to say, "See what it is to be the long-suffering daughter of the greatest genius in the world, and pity me!"

Cosmo Chough had been reading some of his 'Triumph of Womanhood,' lying on the hearth-rug in the studio.

"Do you think he has proposed?" he asked, darting up, with beaming eyes.

"Proposed! I should think so, and been told not to play such tricks again."

"Ah!" cried Chough, "thank heaven. I—I—" but he stopped.

"You shall send Anne your Ginevra in the Tomb, papa, as a wedding present."

"Don't be in too great a hurry," said old Saunders; whereupon he was jeered at with all the respect due to so great an artist.

For the first time after so long, Anne felt happy. A load was off her mind. That Hamlin should love Sacha, and Sacha Hamlin, was the miracle which alone could release her, and releasing her, put an end at the same time to the horrible false position into which Hamlin's self-engagement to a woman so different from himself created for him also in the future. And now only did it strike Anne that perhaps she had no right towards Hamlin to pay off her debt of gratitude at the expense of what might be his future misery as well as hers. Had Hamlin been sufficiently infatuated to wish to marry a woman whom he did not really and solidly love, would it have been right on her part to let him have his way? All these doubts, which she had previously put behind her, as mere selfish sophistry to tempt her from her duty, now rushed home to her. But they came no longer to torment, but to add to the relief, the cessation of bondage. Hamlin would never, she said to herself, have been really happy with her as a wife; and now it happened that he had met the woman who, whatever her shortcomings, seemed to suit him. That Sacha Elaguine was an undisciplined, thoughtless, rather sensuous woman, loving excitement and art, and indifferent to abstract good and evil, Anne fully admitted; but were not these the very qualities which would make her appreciate what in Hamlin was original and charming, and blind her, for her happiness (and added Anne, convinced by sad failure of the futility of trying to change people's nature) and for his, to his weak sides? And Sacha had just that exuberant passionateness, more of the temperament and the fancy than of the heart, which Hamlin required, and which she, Anne, so lamentably lacked. For Sacha also it would mean a new life: it would mean, for the poor, excitable little woman, always defrauded of affection and of an object of adoration, a reality in her life, something to love, to worship, to pet, to flatter—something to make her forget her miserable bedraggled childhood, her wretched married life, her persecution and her maladies. This it would mean to them; and to Anne it would mean . . . Ah! Anne did not dare to think what it would mean for her; she was not yet sure. She might be mistaken, she was still bound to doubt. And still, that great bliss, at which Anne was afraid to look, meant only what to other women would have been a poor gift: liberty to gain her bread, to feel and think for herself—a life's solitude.

Days passed on; and Anne, instead of being, as she expected, disappointed, was confirmed by every little thing in her belief. On one pretext or other, Hamlin was perpetually at Madame Elaguine's. The latest excuse for seeing her was to paint her portrait; so, for a number of days, Sacha came every morning to the house at Hammersmith, and spent a couple of hours at least closeted with Hamlin in the studio. Anne usually received her, and she frequently stayed to lunch; and Miss Brown could not help feeling indignant at the coolness with which Hamlin amused himself playing with two women: he was perpetually trailing after Sacha, he was perpetually, she felt persuaded, talking about life and love and himself in a way which was equivalent to making love to the little woman; and yet, he would still come and sit at Anne's feet, and represent himself as the dejected and heartbroken creature whom only a strong and pure woman could help. Once, Miss Brown had considerable difficulty in restraining herself when, after a day spent with his cousin, he came in the evening to her, and began the usual talk about his soul being shrivelled up.

"I feel I am not worthy to live!" he exclaimed. "I have become too weak and selfish to enjoy the world; I feel that I am sinking into a bog of meanness and sensuality; and yet I cannot even become the mere beast that I ought—the mere beast that would be satisfied with the mud. I keep looking up, and longing for higher things which I cannot attain."

"How very sad!" said Anne, icily; "what a pity you can't make up your mind! it would save you much valuable time. But then, I suppose, it always comes in usefully for sonnets. That is the great advantage of being a poet."

Hamlin was silent. He had—she felt sure, and she was indignant as if at an affront—imagined that he might tempt her into saying—"I will raise you," while his poor, giddy, irresponsible cousin was being dragged further and further into a passion which she would never recover from—for she, at least, had a heart and he had none.

"You despise me!" cried Hamlin, after a minute.

"I thought your indecision between the bog and the stars rather contemptible, certainly, just now. But I now see that such conditions are as necessary to you as a poet as are your lay figures and studio properties to you as a painter. It was my ignorance."

Hamlin fixed his eyes on the ground. He looked very weak and miserable, and like a man who feels that he has dishonoured himself in some way. But to Anne it was all merely a piece of acting—the climax of that long and nauseous comedy of self-reproach and self-sympathising, of pretending to hanker after evil and good, that was equally indifferent to him,—that comedy which had begun long ago in his letters to her at Coblenz, which she had watched with admiration, and love, and agony at first, and with contempt and disgust at last. And she was hardened towards him. She could have said to him—"Go and marry Sacha!" only that at this moment such a notion seemed an insult to his cousin, and that a horrible fear possessed her that he would seize upon that, and try and work her and her anger into this very patchwork of artificial and morbid sentiment over which he was for ever gloating. Once or twice, indeed, it did occur to Anne that perhaps this whole flirtation with Madame Elaguine had been got up by Hamlin for her, benefit; that he was playing with the heart of the foolish little woman (who did not realise that he was making her love him) merely to provoke Anne's jealousy—to move her by this means, since he had failed by every other. But even if it had been thus begun, and Miss Brown shrank from believing that Hamlin would have been so deliberately base, it was clear that the comedy had become reality—that he cared for his cousin and she for him. Perhaps—perhaps—all this remorse was real after all. But Anne's heart had got hardened against him: she could no longer, do what he liked, believe that there was anything genuine in him.

Meanwhile Hamlin's perpetual attendance on Madame Elaguine had become apparent to every one; and even Mrs Spencer admitted to her father that Hamlin could not have proposed that day she had met Anne.

"That is to say—mind you, I daresay he actually did propose; but that wretched woman somehow contrived to talk him over again. I believe she's capable of everything!"

"Well, my dear," said her father, "it goes a little against your theory that Miss Brown looks just as happy as possible."

"Because she's too honourable to believe!" exclaimed Mrs Spencer; and forgetting the many acrimonious remarks in which she had indulged against Miss Brown, and the many times she had sighed at Walter Hamlin taking up with a "mere soulless Italian" instead of with this or the other Sappho or Properzia dei Rossi of her circle, she added—"I always knew that Anne was one of the noblest women in the world; and the nobler women are, the less will they believe in the baseness of men. For my part, I think love and marriage are the greatest curses of a woman's life."

In which sentiment poor Mr Spencer modestly acquiesced.

"I shall have to warn her some day, if no one else has the courage to do so," she said. Of course no one else did have the courage. Edmund Lewis became every day more and more offensive in manner to Miss Brown; he hated her, and he enjoyed seeing her what he considered ousted.

Mrs Macgregor, although she went on abusing Madame Elaguine for being the Sacha of other days, lived too much in her bedroom, saw too little of what was going on even in the house, to guess at anything. Mary and Marjory Leigh looked on in wonder and indignation; but Anne's calm and cheerful manner forbade their saying anything. Did not Anne know better than any one how Hamlin felt towards her? and if Anne was satisfied, must it not all be a delusion?

"Besides, Hamlin is too honourable," said Mary, forgetting about the letter to Harry Collett; "and how could a poet, an artist, prefer an odious, rowdy, hysterical creature like Madame Elaguine to such a being as Anne Brown?" The mere thought seemed a profanation.

"I don't think Hamlin is a bit noble," said Marjory, sternly; "and such a little wretch is just likely to pamper his vanity—and Anne is too honest to do that."

"Every man has a nobler and a baser side," said Harry Collett, mercifully. "Madame Elaguine (though I think it very uncharitable to hate her because she is a little rowdy, and I'm sure she's quite innocent) may flatter Hamlin's worse part. But the nobler will always have its way, and with it Miss Brown. Walter is weak, but he can see the difference between an inferior woman and a superior one. Besides, after all, she is his cousin, and I see no reason to go tittle-tattling because two cousins are friends."

"That's the way Harry pays off Hamlin for writing that beastly letter about me!" said Marjory to her sister, when Mr Collett was gone. "How I do hate evangelical charity! how I do wish Harry had just a little of the bad in him!"

Mary laughed, and catching hold of Marjory, kissed her.

"What do you mean?" cried Marjory, indignantly breaking loose.

"I mean, Marjory dear, that though you imagine the contrary, you are very, very glad that Harry is just what he is."

"Well, perhaps I am. But still, oh, I do hate . . ."

And thus the Leighs, being very happy themselves, forgot Anne Brown's supposed grievances, even as the best of us, being happy, will forget the wrongs of others.

But there was one person who could not forget what seemed to him the most fright− ful sacrilege in the world; and that person was Mr Cosmo Chough. He considered himself as the assistant high priest of the divinity called Anne Brown, and he believed that it was his duty to bring back the high priest in person, namely Hamlin, to the worship from which the powers of evil had momentarily seduced him. But he thought it more simple to apply to the offended goddess than to her recalcitrant priest, who, to tell the truth, had treated his vague remarks with considerable scorn. Accordingly, one day (June had come round now) Miss Brown was informed that Mr Cosmo Chough desired to see her.

"How ao you do, Mr Chough?" said Anne, stretching out her hand to the little man, who came in with even more than usually brushed coat and hat, and more than usually blacked boots, his lips squeezed into a long, cat−like grimace of solemnity, his brows knit gloomily, and walking on the tips of his toes like an operatic conspirator. Mr Chough sat down and sighed.

"Will you have some tea?" asked Miss Brown, with her hand on the bell.

The poet of womanhood darted up, laid one hand lightly on Anne's arm, and opening and straightening out the other with an eloquent gesture, said—

"Excuse me. I would rather have no tea. I want your attention—your *best* attention—seriously and at once."

Anne could not help smiling.

"You can have both some tea and my best, my very best attention," she said.

Mr Chough sighed, and waited gloomily until tea had been brought, absolutely refusing to open his lips.

"Have you brought something to read to me?" asked Anne, thinking it might be some new bit of the 'Triumph of Womanhood,' which Cosmo Chough most innocently read to all the ladies of his acquaintance, only Anne having the courage to say every now and then, "I think that had better be omitted, Mr Chough. I think people will give it a bad meaning which perhaps you don't intend."

"I have nothing to read," answered Chough, solemnly. "I have come to ask your advice about a matter more important than any literary one."

"You shall have it if I can give any. Go on, Mr Chough."

"Well, then," began Cosmo, stooping forward on his chair and frowning, "let me premise that I have two friends whom I greatly value. I am not at liberty to mention their names; but I will call one the Duke, and the other la Marquise."

"Oh!" cried Anne, laughing, "I fear I can't give you any advice about such exalted people as that. I am a woman of the people, and have never known a duke in my life."

"One moment's patience, dear Miss Brown. This Duke—who lives—well, let us say he has a magnificent *hôtel entre cour et jardin* in Paris, has been affianced ever since his childhood to the Marquise, who is the most beau– tiful and divine woman in the world, as he, indeed, is the most accomplished gentleman, besides being my dearest friend; and they have been looking forward to a union which will make their happiness, and that of their friends, perfect. Do you follow that? But now—" and Cosmo Chough, stretching out one long thin leg, so as to display his small foot and the martial wrinkles of his boot, and propping his elbow on his other knee—"now, mark. There comes into our perfect duet a discordant voice. A certain lady, whom I will designate as the Queen of Night"—and he made his cat's grimace, and pausing, looked mournfully at Miss Brown, who sat quietly by, bending over a piece of embroidery which she was doing from a design by Hamlin.

"Well!"

"Well, this lady, by some occult power of which I cannot judge, gains possession of the fancy of the Duke—not of his heart,—he still continuing to love the Marquise *coralment*, as the *trouvères* say,—and in short leads him, without however, as I said, in the least diminishing his passionate love for the Marquise, into acts, or at least appearances, which, to the mind of the vulgar are incompatible with such love. What do you say to that?"

Little by little Miss Brown had guessed what Chough was hiding beneath this grotesque piece of romancing.

"I say that the vulgar are probably right; and that the Marquise, for all the *coral* love of the Duke, had better throw him over, if she has a grain of self-respect. Will you have another cup, Mr Chough?"

Anne spoke coldly and indifferently; and Chough, who, despite his vaunted knowledge of the human heart, was the most obtuse of good-hearted little people, actually prided himself upon having put his case so delicately, that Miss Brown could not even guess as yet that she was alluded to.

"But the Duke would die were he to lose her! The Queen of Night, who is a wicked fairy—*une méchante fée*—*une fernme serpent*—*une mélusine, enfin tout ce qu'il vous plaira*" (Chough always liked to show off his French)—"has fascinated only his fancy, not his heart. It would be most unfair if he were to lose the Marquise. Well, to proceed; the remedy would easily be found. La Marquise, like all passionately loving women, is a little cold and proud—*tant soit peu hautaine et glaciale*—need only thaw towards the Duke. She need only say or make a friend tell him, that she adores him and that he is her sole happiness—and see! the Queen of Night's spells are forthwith broken by the power of true love—the Eternal Womanhood reasserts its right, and all is happy again. But the mischief is, that there is no means of bringing this home to the lady. Lately, indeed, a trusty and respectful friend, an Italian—a poet of some small distinction, I may add—ventured so far as to acquaint her of the public rumour concerning—I mean concerning the Duke and the Queen of Night—in an anonymous letter . . ."

Miss Brown suddenly sat bolt-upright, and fixing her eyes on Chough, said—

"You don't mean to say that you—you actually concocted that ridiculous missive?"

"Ridiculous missive! What ridiculous missive?" asked Cosmo Chough, striking an attitude.

"Well, I ought rather to say that most ungentlemanly anonymous letter, written in Italian which would make a cat laugh."

"Ungentlemanly! ungentlemanly!" howled Chough; but in reality what he was thinking of was Miss Brown's stricture upon the Italian.

"Oh, Miss Brown!" he cried, after a minute, "and it is possible that you should so far have misunderstood the friend who respects you most in the whole world, as to have supposed that that letter had any evil intention? Is it possible that you, who have of all people in the world been kindest to me, who have been as a mother to my children—that you should have such an opinion of me?"

Poor Cosmo had let go all his affectation; he wrung his hands in real distress, and he actually seemed to be crying.

"Oh fool, fool that I was, trying to do good, and merely making myself seem an odious ungrateful wretch!"

His sorrow was so genuine that Miss Brown felt quite sorry for him.

"Come, come, dear Mr Chough," she said, "don't distress yourself. I think you did a rather improper thing, but I am quite persuaded that you merely wished to do good."

And she stretched out her hand.

Chough struck his head with his fist.

"Ah, you are good—you are *too* good—dear, dear Miss Brown! but I shall never recover from it—never. To think I only wished to do good—and you think me a slanderer!"

"Oh no," said Anne, quietly, "I don't think it for a moment. I know that all that letter contained was true, except that you were unjust to one of the parties; for I am sure Madame Elaguine is not at all base, and has no conception of what she is drifting into."

Chough gaped in astonishment.

"You believe it to be true, and yet . . ."

"How can I help believing by this time what every creature can see, and what every creature, except themselves perhaps, must and does see as clear as the sun at noon?"

Anne spoke very composedly.

"But if that is the case—if you know—why then, how is it that you don't—well, that you don't put a stop to it?"

"One can't put a stop to what has already taken place."

"Oh, but you can—you can—and it was in hopes of your doing it that I wrote that letter. It is to entreat you to do it that I have come now, dear, dear Miss Brown, to supplicate, to implore you . . ."

"To do what?" There was a freezing indifference in her voice.

"To do what? Why, to do everything and anything! Dearest Miss Brown, I know, I understand fully, that Hamlin has acted unworthily towards you. I know, I admit, that to a woman like you—all passion, all nobility—Hamlin's behaviour must be odious. But would it not be worthy of you to reflect that Hamlin is a poet, and acting merely as a poet must act? A poet is a double-natured creature, a baser and a nobler nature, and his whole life consists merely in receiving as many and various impressions as both his natures can receive. A poet must know the stars, and know the mud beneath his feet; he must drink the milk and the absinthe of life,—he must love purely and impurely, with his heart, with his fancy, and with his senses—ah, you frown!—well, but such the poet is, such is

Hamlin. His soul loves and adores you; what if, at the same time, his baser nature, the satyr in the god, be caught elsewhere? He loves you none the less; yes, he loves you even at the moment . . ."

"I think this all rather disgusting, don't you, Mr Chough?" said Anne, sternly.

"Nay, have patience—for the sake of Hamlin, for the sake of your own noble good-ness! He loves you: and it requires but a look, a word, a message, to make him forget that other love, to make it evaporate like opium-fumes. Oh say this word—say it—and blow that ugly cloud of impure love from off the fair resplendent face of his devotion to you! Write to him—speak to him. Empower me, oh dearest lady, to tell him that you love him, and that this wretched fancy of his is making you miserable!"

"It is not," answered Anne, harshly; "it is not doing anything of the sort, and it is no more a fancy than his love for me. As to Madame Elaguine, she is in every way fit to be his wife."

"His wife!" screamed Chough, and looked as if he would faint; "and you would let your resentment go thus far—you would let the nettles choke the roses, the impure passion choke the pure one, you would sacrifice him and yourself—you would let him . . ."

"I would let him marry his cousin. There is no impurity about it, so please don't revert to that, Mr Chough. She is just the woman who might make him happy; the inclination is perfectly natural and proper."

Chough started up. "Oh, you saint! you noble heroic woman!" he cried, kissing Anne's dress enthusiastically.

"What are you doing, Mr Chough?" she asked angrily.

"I am kissing the holiest thing I shall ever touch," answered the little man solemnly. "Yes! you are a saint, an Alkertis, an Iphigenia! But we will not let the monstrous self-sacrifice take place! No, by heaven! never, never! You shall not give up your happiness; I will speak to Hamlin. I will tell him all, all—that you love him . . ."

"I do not love Hamlin," said Anne sternly, pronouncing every word clearly and slowly.

"You do not love Hamlin!—you do not want—"

Poor little Chough was so utterly dumfounded that he had not the breath to finish his sentence.

"You have obliged me to say what I never intended to say to any one," said Anne. "No; I do not love Hamlin; and if he marry his cousin, I shall be happier than I thought I ever could be."

"You love another!" whispered Chough, his eyebrows and whiskers standing on end.

"Neither him nor any one else."

"Then why—why have you not told him so? Why make the sacrifice of your inclinations—because, marrying him, you would be—why?"

"Mr Hamlin has done everything for me. I was a penniless, ignorant servant. He had me taught, he gave me his money, he gave me more kindness and trustfulness and generosity than any man ever gave any woman I think, and I must pay my debt. If he wants me, he shall have me. If not, so much the better for me."

There was a silence. Anne took up her piece of work; Chough sat rapping gently on the table with his finger-tips, looking wonderingly at her.

At last Miss Brown spoke.

"You have got my secret out of me, Mr Chough. I don't believe much in you poets; and I think you are a giddy, often a foolish man. But I think you are a gentleman at heart, and a good man; and as such, I trust you never to let out, either by speech or hint or look, positively or negatively, a word of what I have told you. If Mr Hamlin marry his cousin, so much the better; if he marry me, so much the worse. But what must be, must be. And come what may, I depend upon you, as the only friend upon whom I can rely, to forget all that I have told you to-day. Will you promise?"

Miss Brown looked very solemn; and Chough was overcome by an almost religious awe.

"I promise never to reveal," he said quietly, "but you must not ask me to forget; I have neither the power nor the right to forget the best thing I have known in my life. Goodbye, Miss Brown, and God bless you!"

And Anne, who believed only in right and wrong, felt really the better and stronger for the blessing of the preposterous little poet of Messalina and Lucrezia Borgia, who declared himself to be an atheist when he did not declare himself to be a Catholic mystic.

CHAPTER VII.

SOME time after this conversation with Cosmo Chough, a circumstance took place which caused great momentary excitement, and considerably unsettled Miss Brown's mind. The summer had come with a sudden rush; and Hamlin had had the notion of taking his aunt and Miss Brown, and two or three friends, to spend a week at Wotton. Among these friends was Madame Elaguine. That Hamlin should care to take his cousin to the house where she had played so lamentable a part in her childhood; that Sacha should endure to confront those invisible ghosts of her uncle, her cousins, her own former self, of all the shameful past, which haunted that house, was quite incomprehen- sible to Anne. But day by day she was forced to recognise that she was surrounded by incomprehensible ways of feeling and thinking, that she was, in a way, like a person solitary among mankind from deafness or blindness, from incapacity to put herself in their place; and recognising this, she recognised also, with her unflinching justice, that she had no right to hastily condemn the things which she could not understand. So when Madame Elaguine, on the evening of her arrival at Wotton, insisted on wandering all over the once familiar house, and openly said that she felt a pleasure, the bitter pleasure of self-inflicted penance, in confronting the past, in humiliating her present self by the company of her former self, Anne merely said to herself that she could not conceive a woman feeling like that—but that, nevertheless, this theatrical and hysterical excitement might, after all, lead to as good a result as her own silent and painful solitary self-absorption.

"She is a brazen creature!" Aunt Claudia had cried, when she heard that Sacha was going to Wotton; "corrupt like her father, and fantastic like her mother. She must get Mrs Spencer or some one else to chaperon her in that house, if indeed she wants any one. I shall stay behind. As to you, Annie, you are at liberty to go or not go, of course."

"I shall go, Aunt Claudia," Anne had answered resolutely, "because I don't see that I have a right to imply by my absence that I disapprove of Madame Elaguine's going to Wotton. I neither approve nor disapprove; and I think that, however little we may sympathise with her notions of self-humiliation, we must give her the benefit of supposing that she is honest in them."

So Anne had gone.

The self-humiliation of Madame Elaguine, and the hours she had spent in her room—she had asked for the room which had been hers as a child—crying over the past, did not prevent her being in excessively high spirits the evening following their arrival and the successive one. It would seem as if the painful associations in which she had steeped herself had produced a reaction in her whole nature. She was childishly, almost uproariously gay, played with little Helen the greater part of the afternoon, and after dinner treated the company—that is to say, Anne, Mrs Spencer, Lewis, and Hamlin—to a perfect concert of all manner of wild gipsy songs, Spanish and Russian, sung with a fury which amounted almost to genius; and followed these up with little French songs, old and new, picked up heaven knows where—from operettes, from peasants, from books—the words of which and the astonishing *gaminerie* with which they were delivered, amused Lewis to fits of laughing, threw Chough into enthusiasm, annoyed Hamlin a little, puzzled poor Mrs Spencer, and made Anne reflect, as charitably as she could, upon the different standards of propriety which seemed to exist for Englishwomen and for Russians.

Madame Elaguine's songs made Anne feel quite uncomfortable and angry; but she said nothing, seeing Mrs Spencer, who could tolerate any amount of impropriety as long as it was medieval and poetic, was evidently putting down this French levity as a mark of the Russian woman's depravity; and she felt somehow, that though she was annoyed herself, and annoyed with good cause, she must not back up Mrs Spencer's prejudiced indignation.

Cousin Sacha seemed to take a pleasure in vexing Hamlin, in shocking Anne, in making Mrs Spencer think her a wicked creature; she sang on, in her devil-may-care, street-boy way, with a malicious, childish impudence in her face; then suddenly, when she saw Hamlin get positively black at what he considered her bad taste—suddenly dropped from her *leste* French couplets into a strange, wild, Spanish gipsy song, sad and despairing beyond saying.

She looked very fascinating, as she sat near the window, resting her guitar on her knee, her tiny feet and embroidered stockings very visible beneath the lace flounces and frills of her thistle-down dress; her deep, Russian blue eyes looking, as it seemed, rather into the past than the present, her whole slight, even emaciated, body and face tense with a sort of hysterical emotion.

Suddenly she threw the guitar on the sofa.

"Bah!" she cried, "what is the use of singing sad things when one is sad? and what is the use of pretending to be merry, and shocking people with *polissoneries* when one feels as old and dismal as at ninety? I hate music."

And she walked through the French window on to the wide terrace which surrounded one side of the house and overlooked the lawn.

"The only good thing," she said, "in this world is tobacco-smoke. If," turning with affected deference and timidity to Mrs Spencer, who considered a woman who smoked as little short of an adventuress, "you have no objection, these gentlemen and I will have a smoke."

"Oh, pray don't mind me," snorted Mrs Spencer, stalking back into the drawing-room, and sitting down near the window.

The three men immediately produced cigars and cigarettes and matches.

"No, thank you, Walter," said Madame Elaguine; "your cigarettes are too weak for me—too ladylike, like their owner, for a badly brought up woman. I must make mine myself." And she went into her bedroom, the last room opening out to the terrace, to fetch her box of tobacco and her cigarette-papers.

In a minute she returned, whistling, in a curious bird-like whistle, below her breath, and rolling a cigarette in her fingers. Some of the party were seated, some standing. Madame Elaguine came to where Miss Brown was seated, looking into the twilight park.

"Dear Annie," she murmured, putting her arm round Miss Brown's neck, in her childish way, and which yet always affected Anne as might the caress of a lamia's clammy scales.

"I fear," she said, putting her face close to Anne, and lowering her voice to a whisper, "that you must have thought me horribly vulgar and undignified and indecent just now. I don't know why I sang all those nasty songs; I suppose it was to vex Walter. I don't like them myself. But sometimes a sort of horrible desire, a kind of demon inside me, makes me wish to do something which I know is disgusting; I feel as if I could be the lowest of women, just from perversity. Ah, it is sickening."

Anne did not answer.

"Where did you learn those wonderful little Burgundian couplets, Sacha?" asked Lewis, in his sultan-like familiar way. He had a trick of calling her Sacha every now and then, as he had tried, but failed, to call Miss Brown Annie.

"I don't know. I ought not to have learned them at all; and I ought not to have sung them before a man like you, who notices all the nastiness there is in anything, and a great deal more besides," answered Madame Elaguine, coldly.

"What a Southern evening!" exclaimed Cosmo Chough, looking up at the blue evening sky, singularly pure and blue and high, twinkling with stars, and against which the distant trees stood out clear like the sidescenes of a theatre. "It is sad that our cigars should have to do for fireflies,—to be the only thing imitating that," and he pointed at the sky.

"A lit cigar is the only imitation of the stars which people like ourselves can attempt," said the Russian. "It's so in everything—our poetry, our passions—nothing but cigar-lights for stars; don't you think so, Annie?"

"What's that?" asked Chough, suddenly.

They looked up at his startled voice.

"What's what?" asked Madame Elaguine, quietly. "Have you seen the ghost of Imperia of Rome, Mr Chough?"

"What the deuce is that?" exclaimed Lewis. In the midst of the general blue dusk, one of the cedars on the lawn, and a screen of trees beyond, had suddenly burst into sight, enveloped in a bright light, which made the grass all round burn out a vivid yellowish–green against the darkness.

Anne turned round quickly and looked behind her.

"The house is on fire!" she cried. "Madame Elaguine's room!" And before the others could understand, she had rushed towards the other end of the terrace.

The light, which had suddenly illumined the piece of lawn, the trees opposite, did issue, a brilliant broad sheet like that of large chandelier, from out of the open window of Sacha's room.

"Good heavens!" cried Hamlin, "you must have set the curtains on fire with the match of your cigarette!"

"No, no," cried Madame Elaguine, "I lit my cigarette here outside; it must be . . ." and she rushed wildly after Anne into her bedroom.

An extraordinary spectacle met Miss Brown first, and the rest of the party an instant or two later.

The large old–fashioned bed of Cousin Sacha, which stood in the centre of the room, was burning, blazing like a Christmas pudding, its whole top, coverlet and pillows, turned into a roaring mass of bluish flame, whence arose an acrid stifling smell.

"They have done it! they have done it!" shrieked Madame Elaguine, throwing herself into Hamlin's arms. "They want to kill me! they have always said so!"

But before he had had time to answer, she had rushed off into a neighbouring room, and, with a presence of mind most unexpected in her, returned with a heap of woollen blankets which she had dragged off a bed.

"Pour the water on this!" she cried to Anne, who, with her strong arms, had immediately dashed the contents of a bath on to the flames. "Soak this! it is useless throwing water on the flames;" and taking the soaking blankets, the little woman threw them dexterously on to the blazing bed, among the hissing of the smoke and fire.

In a minute every one had brought blankets, cushions, water; the servants had run up; and in about five minutes the flames were extinguished.

The damages were very trifling compared with the appearance of danger. The fire had not spread beyond the surface of the bed, and consumed only the upper layer of bedding. But the sight of that expanse of waving blue flame had been frightful, and it seemed impossible to realise that no harm had been done.

"How has it happened?"—"How have they done it?"—"Send to the police station."—"Scour the park!"—every one was talking at the same time.

"I'll go down into the park and have a good hunt," said Hamlin, taking down one of the guns which hung in the hall; "they can't have got far yet."

"I don't think you'll catch them," answered Lewis, in his drawling ironical way.

"We're not in Russia, Mr Lewis," rejoined Mrs Spencer, bridling up; "**here** any one can be caught; it's not an incompetent police as abroad."

"Some things can't be caught," said Lewis, with an odd wise smile.

While they were standing discussing in the hall, they were startled by a sudden thump on the floor. Madame Elaguine, who had hitherto been singularly calm and energetic, had fallen in a half-fainting condition, like a column on to the ground. She was carried in to a couch in the drawing-room, and Anne called the Swiss maid, who came, with that sort of insolent indifference to the condition of her mistress, which had struck Miss Brown on more than one similar occasion. Madame Elaguine was in a state of hysterical panic—she wept, and laughed, and talked, and moaned; but she absolutely refused to be put to bed, and insisted with great violence that some of the company should remain about her. She kept Hamlin seated by the side of the sofa, his hand in hers, until the arrival of the police, and of neighbours who had heard of the burning bed, obliged him and the men to leave her. As soon as only Mrs Spencer and Anne Brown remained, she became more calm, and merely lamented over her fate, and over the probability that some day her enemies would really succeed in killing either her or her child.

A curious coincidence occurred, which remained impressed in Anne's mind. While the rest of the party, including Mrs Spencer, were examining the house in company with the policemen, Miss Brown, who was seated near Madame Elaguine's sofa—a sense of unreality, as of being at the play, filling her whole nature after that terrible sight of the blazing bed—mechanically opened a book which was lying on the table at her elbow. It was a child's story which she had bought on a railway bookstall and given to little Helen Ela- guine to keep her quiet during the journey to Wotton. Mechanically her eye ran along the page; but suddenly it stopped, as she read the following sentence, printed in rather larger type than the rest—

"And they never forgot, as long as they lived, that terrible burning bed."

For a moment the words echoed through Anne's mind as merely so much sound; but, as is the case when we hear a name which awakens associations which we cannot at first define to ourselves, she was conscious at the same time of an effort to adjust her faculties, to seize a meaning which was there, but which she could not at once grasp.

"And they never forgot, as long as they lived, that terrible burning bed."

Anne kept on repeating those words to herself. They made her restless. She went to the window, and looked out into the night. The vision of that broad sheet of white light on the terrace and bushes, of that expanse of waving blue flamelets, rose up in her mind.

"That terrible burning bed." She saw the printed page again. Then, as to a central bubble, other ideas which bubbled up slowly began to gravitate. Madame Elaguine's perfect, and, in a woman so excitable, unaccountable presence of mind until all chance of further mischief had been over; the blankets which she had immediately dragged out of the next room, as a fireman might have dragged them; the rapid instruction, as of a person accustomed to such things, to wet the blankets instead of pouring water on the flames, as all the others had done; the insolent, indifferent look of the maid; the going into her room to fetch the cigarette-papers only a minute or two before the conflagration, and when it would seem that whoever had set the bed aflame must have been making the necessary preparations. Then also, the fire had been so carefully limited to the bed, as if no real damage had been meant. No; that was merely consistent with the usual policy of Madame Elaguine's mysterious enemies, who wished to frighten, but not to kill her. But another thought arose. Madame Elaguine possessed a good deal of valuable old lace, indeed more than her fortune at all warranted. Old lace was her hobby and her pride; she had always a lot on her dress, on her night-gown, on everything. Some of the very finest that she possessed existed in large quantity as the trimming of a white satin dressing-gown, which, towards the evening, was always put on her bed. Anne had noticed it this very evening, when Madame Elaguine had called her into her bedroom to ask her advice, as, with a spoilt child's coquetry, she often did, about some flowers which she was putting in her hair for dinner. For some reason the maid had already arranged the room for the night, and, as usual, the white satin dressing-gown trimmed with lace had been lying on the bed. Anne had made a note of the fact, because she had thought at the moment how absurd it was of the Russian to put such valuable lace upon a garment which was perpetually knocking about, and in which, as it seemed to Miss Brown, she would scarcely be seen except by her own servant. Now, while extinguishing the flames, one of Anne's first thoughts had somehow been the white satin dressing-gown. What a pity that all that lace should have been consumed! What an annoyance to Cousin Sacha! But, to her surprise and relief, she had seen the dressing-gown, a mass of satin and lace, hanging in perfect safety on a peg at the furthest end of the room—the dressing-gown which, an hour before, had already lain in readiness on the bed.

All these ideas moved confusedly through Miss Brown's brain. Was it a mere ordinary mental delusion, one of those impressions which physiologists explain by the imperfect momentary double action of the two brain-lobes; or was it a recollection of a suspicion which had long existed in her mind, but unconsciously, not daring to come to the surface? Anyhow, it seemed to Anne, as she stood by the open window looking into the night, and listening to Sacha's faint moanings, as if she had gone through that or something similar before—as if it were not the first time that she was invaded by the thought that all this persecution by invisible and uncatchable enemies was a deception practised by Madame Elaguine herself, a kind of artificial excitement and interest got up for the benefit of her friends, for the benefit of her own morbid and theatrical temper? It was difficult for a woman, simple, sincere, completely all of a piece, like Anne Brown, to conceive such a possibility, and still more difficult for her not to revolt from its contemplation as from an act of disloyalty. But, on the other hand, Anne, just in proportion to her slowness of mental perception, had not the power, which so many of us possess, of denying the evidence of her reason for the sake of her feelings. So the words in the book, which seemed as if they contained the suggestion of the whole performance (if performance it was); the fact of the dressing-gown having been out of reach of all danger; the manner of Madame Elaguine and of her maid on this and previous occasions,—haunted Anne, and united with the sudden recollection of what she had read in one of Marjory Leigh's scientific books about the connection between hysteria and monomania, about the strange passion for deceit, for hoax, for theatricality, sometimes observable in hysterical women. And then she remembered the face and voice of Edmund Lewis, his ironical remark about the impossibility of finding the culprits, his indifference and amused superiority. Could he too have guessed?—and, it suddenly struck her, could Hamlin have had the same thought? No, she felt sure Hamlin had not.

BOOK VIII.

CHAPTER I.

THE incident of the burning bed left the inmates of Wotton Hall in a state of excitement which outlasted their stay in the country. All attempts to find the culprits had been useless; and Madame Elaguine had begged Hamlin not to permit any regular judicial inquiry, lest the story of her persecution, about which she affected to be excessively jealous, should become public property. Hamlin, who hated vulgar publicity, easily consented. But the mysterious story was now known to all the guests at Wotton, and soon became known to the whole pre-Raphaelite set which centred round the house at Hammersmith, with the result of turning Madame Elaguine, in the eyes of Mrs Spencer and her friends, from something not much better than an adventuress, into something uncommonly like a heroine and a martyr; for it seemed as if these good folk, whose life was the most humdrum prose and whose ideal was the most far-fetched poetry, felt absolute gratitude towards the remarkable individual who supplied them with a real mystery, a real persecution by unknown enemies, a real romance. So when Sacha, on her return to town, began to suffer or to think that she suffered from nervous prostration due to this terrible shock, and to lie even more than usual on sofas in even more than usually picturesque dressing–gowns, she found herself surrounded by a crowd of sympathising and admiring artists, writers, and critics, to whom she confided, one by one, and in slightly different versions, the details of her strange history.

The only person who seemed displeased was Hamlin; and the only person who seemed cold was Miss Brown. Hamlin always required to absorb the whole attention of any person to whom he took a liking; to see his cousin fenced round with idiots, as he described it, was almost a physical annoyance to him; he was cross, captious, bitter, and gruff; and the more he showed his temper the more pleasure Madame Elaguine took in provoking him. As usual, when out of sorts with the world, and especially when he felt himself neglected, Hamlin began once more to pay attentions to Miss Brown, to bemoan his own baseness and weakness, to throw himself on her compassion, to insinuate that in her lay his only hope.

This sort of talk, with his beautiful dreamy eyes fixed adoringly upon her, his slow quiet voice sounding like that of a votary before an altar, had long become for Anne a mere additional bitterness; a bitterness of comprehension proportionate to the long delusion which had made her see in this sort of behaviour the dissatisfaction of a noble nature, the yearnings of real love. She was accustomed to it; and would have merely smiled the bitter smile which had become part of her nature. But now, every lover–like look or word from Ham- lin inspired Anne with positive terror; it seemed as if he had let her fancy that he loved his cousin—that he had let her dream of release, of freedom from the life captivity which threatened her soul, only to creep back, as a cat creeps back to the mouse with which it is playing, and slowly stretch forth his hand to seize her. This feeling became so strong in Anne that little by little there developed in her a nervous dread of Hamlin: every time that he approached her alone, that he fixed his eyes on her face or addressed her by her name, she was aware of a chill throughout her body, of a sudden pallor in her face; a chill, a pallor which, if noticed, must mean to Hamlin that she loved him.

Into this vague and painful suspense were vaguely mingled the suspicions which she had formed regarding Madame Elaguine. Confusedly Anne was conscious that the worthiness or unworthiness of Sacha was not a matter of indifference to her; if Sacha was a mere hysterical liar, she could not sincerely love Hamlin, Hamlin could not love her; and if this man and this woman did not love one another, Anne Brown was once more, what she had for a brief time imagined that she was no longer, the slave of her protector, as Mademoiselle Aïssé had been the slave of M. de Ferréol.

Suddenly, one day, there came a change, and with it the end of the terrible doubt and fear which were corroding Miss Brown's soul. What had happened Anne never clearly understood; she only perceived a change, and guessed that it was connected in some manner with the sudden disappearance of Edmund Lewis, and with some tremendous quarrel between him and Hamlin which seemed to have preceded it. Mr Lewis, who had spent all his mornings in Hamlin's studio, and all his evenings in Madame Elaguine's boudoir, appeared to have sunk into the ground; his very name was scarcely mentioned; and Anne Brown, who hated the very sight of the little man with the sealing-wax lips and green cat-like eyes, who instinctively felt that he personified all the peculiarities which degraded Hamlin in her eyes, had a vague superstitious notion that now that he was gone everything would settle happily.

What had Lewis done? Had he insulted Madame Elaguine; and had this insulting, by a man who was his friend, of a woman whom he loved, made Hamlin suddenly conscious of his love for Sacha, and of his duty to protect an irresponsible little woman whom his indecision was putting into a false position? The more Miss Brown pored over the subject, the more did it seem as if there could be no other explanation.

But whatever the explanation, the result was unmistakable. On the score of ill-health, Madame Elaguine had more or less dismissed all those admiring and sympathising friends who had given Hamlin so much umbrage, and Hamlin had become almost her sole and constant visitor. He appeared to have almost taken up his abode at the Russian's. He came to Hammersmith for lunch as usual, but always found some excuse or other for leaving immediately after: he was painting a portrait of his cousin, and his cousin was too delicate to give him sittings except in her drawing-room. He not merely neglected Anne, but obviously avoided her. He seemed to dread being left alone with her, as much as she, for such very different reasons, had dreaded to be left alone with him: when he did not succeed in getting away, he was moody and depressed; yet he seemed moody and depressed also whenever, as was frequently the case, he was sent for by his cousin, and whenever Anne met them together.

It seemed to Miss Brown as if she could understand it all so well: she, who was slow in understanding others, felt as if she knew Hamlin's character as her own father must have known the construction and working of the machines which she remembered seeing him continually taking to pieces and setting up again. Hamlin had been, so Anne thought, obliged to admit to himself that he loved his cousin, and that he had made her love him;

and he was depressed and irritated at his own inability to take any decided course, at his humiliation in finding that this was the end of all his romance with Anne, at his dread of being obliged, sooner or later, to tell Anne the truth; nay, Miss Brown thought she knew Hamlin sufficiently well to be persuaded that there entered into his feelings a certain annoyance at having to forfeit the exotic and unhealthy pleasure of being partially in love with two women at a time, and at the impetuosity of Sacha precipitating matters from a position of hesitation and self-reproach, which was in some ways pleasant to his peculiar temper, into a situation requiring a definite and prompt solution.

Oh, Anne had not suffered silently these two years, without getting to understand the strange character to which her suffering was due. Yes, she knew Hamlin and what was passing in his mind; and the sense of power implied in this knowledge, the power of following all that he felt and thought, gave her a sort of pleasure, proportionate to that very sense of her difficulty in understanding any character save her own; a curious rare pleasure, in which mingled the consciousness of the price at which it had been bought, and the almost ineffable consciousness that this that she was studying concerned her no more; the pleasure, so often talked about, of the man who has escaped the shipwreck and looks down upon the dangerous waters in safety. Yes; she was safe; she was free.

It gave her a morbid pleasure also to watch Madame Elaguine, who, in the last month or so, ever since the quarrel with Edmund Lewis and the consequent intimacy with her cousin, had suddenly changed in her manner towards Anne—had shown a half-savage, half-childish desire to parade her conquest before her rival, to let her see how completely she had taken Hamlin away from her, to humiliate and insult her: the flaunting perversity of a new sultana towards an old one. Anne had hitherto in- sisted on thinking that Madame Elaguine was really a very noble little woman, and this revelation of a base wish to wound and humiliate, hurt her at first like some nauseous smell arising suddenly beneath her nostrils. But disgust was soon replaced by that new and secret pleasure in the consciousness of understanding this woman better than she understood herself; by the pleasure in feeling how wasted were all Madame Elaguine's insults—how startled would not the little woman be, could she but know that every proof of her supremacy over Hamlin was to Miss Brown as each successively sawed-through window-bar is to the prisoner pining for the day of deliverance.

Anne felt herself getting into so singular a condition of excitement, losing so completely, under the pressure of these conflicting doubts and hopes in the past, of the great joy in the present, all her usual self-composure and self-control, that she took fiercely to working, to hurrying in every way through those studies which she had long since begun in the sickening often-deferred hope that they might become her livelihood if she should ever be released from Hamlin. Miss Brown had often and often, even when the sense of hopelessness had been bitterest, consoled herself with what she believed to be unrealisable dreams for the future; and after going through many possible plans, she had decided that if—if—she should ever become her own mistress, she would employ, resolutely determined to return it to him some day, part of the money which Hamlin had settled upon her, in entering Girton or Newnham, where she would train herself to become a teacher in a public school. Almost mechanically, her studies (and restlessness, and the desire for something that should not be the harassing reality, had developed in her a perfect passion for study) fell into this programme. She had gone in for political economy, history, and what people are pleased to call moral sciences.

Now that liberty seemed on the point of being realised, and that she felt the want of something to steady her shaken nature, she applied herself to this work with redoubled ardour.

"If you go on like that you will get seedy, Annie," warned the practical Marjory Leigh, now on the eve of becoming Mrs Harry Collett.

And Marjory Leigh proved right. The secret excitement of the last months, joined to the recent overwork, was too much for Anne. One day she was suddenly taken ill, and a little time later she was delirious.

"Nervous prostration from overwork," said the doctors.

A great remorse, which was at the same time a great triumph, rose up in Hamlin's heart.

"Sacha," he cried, one day as Madame Elaguine came into the studio at Hammersmith, after visiting the sick woman, "it is I who am killing Anne; and it is you—you—who are forcing me to do it,"—and he tore the portrait of Madame Elaguine off the board of his easel, and pulled the paper, in long ribbons, through his fingers.

"It's no great harm," said the Russian, quietly; "I'm not quite such a guy as you represented me, Watty, and I'm the better pleased not to go down to posterity like that. As to Anne, don't flatter yourself you are breaking her heart, for the excellent reason that there is none to break. Too much study! the doctor says, and he knows. A woman like that works only with her brain. Too much Euclid, Kant, Hegel, Fichte, &c. You needn't flatter yourself that *you* are of the company. Seriously, can you be such a baby as to imagine that if that woman loved you she wouldn't have turned me out of doors ages ago? Besides, she talked only of Girton College and of her cousin Richard when she was delirious, the nurse tells me."

Madame Elaguine watched Hamlin as she let these words drop, then she burst out laughing.

"Poor Walter! what a misfortune it is to be a poet and to be vain! I am really grieved for you. But sooner or later you would understand that when a woman has no heart, but only 'a muscle for pumping the blood to the extremities,' as one of her professors calls it, she can't love; and that, moreover, no woman will ever understand or love you, you silly person, except your cousin Sacha."

Cosmo Chough, who had come to the studio door, and, not being troubled with scruples when base creatures like Madame Elaguine were concerned, and having, moreover, a violent curiosity about everything concerning the Eternal Feminine, had listened at the keyhole, affirmed to Miss Brown some time after that Madame Elaguine had then and there put her arms round Hamlin's neck, and called him a poor, vain little baby.

CHAPTER II.

ON recovering from that long delirium, during which she had raved only about the past and the future, about Miss Curzon, the Perrys, the Villa Arnolfini, Cousin Dick, Girton College, and political economy, but never—by some singular obliviousness of the present—about Hamlin and Sacha,—the first persons that Anne Brown recognised about her were the Leigh girls. Marjory had postponed her marriage in order to help her sister in nursing Miss Brown; and Mrs Macgregor had gladly accepted their proposal to settle for the time being in the house at Hammersmith, she herself being far too unpractical to be of any use. Anne's impressions were vague, diffuse; the ideas aud sensations, the slight amount of life of one day of early convalescence being, so to speak, diluted into what were really days and weeks, day and night succeeding each other confusedly to the girl, but feebly awake and for ever falling asleep. It was a dream, but a pleasant one, consisting of veiled misty impressions, separated by tracts of lethargy: impressions of the kind faces and voices of Mary and Marjory, of the gleams of sunshine on the carpet, of the waving of treetops outside the window, of the whistle of the steamboat on the Thames; the song of the canary in the housekeeper's room—the cry of the milkman; of the bunches of big red and yellow roses put down upon the sheet before her; of the broth and jelly and tea feebly refused, and yet greedily swallowed,—trifles, nothings, but transformed by the haze of mixed weakness and relief into things possessing a charm, and never to be forgotten.

The mere sense of rest and renovation constituted a sort of happiness, with which mingled the consciousness of the kindness of those round her,—of the Leigh girls and Mrs Macgregor, who were in her room nearly all day; of Mrs Spencer, who came from the other end of London every afternoon; of Chough and Cousin Dick, who came to make inquiries; even of Hamlin, whose magnificent bundles and baskets of flowers and fruit arrived regularly, together with the bunch of sweet-peas and pinks which Chough had bought at the greengrocer's, or the sprigs of laburnum which he had stolen in the park. Everything in the world seemed so good and simple; all worries and doubts had gone with the dreadful visions of the delirious nights. Anne had never in her life felt so simply, completely happy; perhaps because, with her tense and tragic character, perfect happiness was possible only in weakness and vagueness.

Little by little the past became concrete once more; but it became concrete as the past, all her doubts and difficulties remaining far distant behind her, like the Alps which the traveller has arduously crossed, and looks back upon from the warm Lombard plain. She took up her position and feelings where she had left them: she felt herself free. At first she could scarcely tell why, as we sometimes can scarcely account to ourselves for something which has happened the previous day, and which, though forgotten, fills us with vague pleasure or pain on awakening. Then she began to understand once more, and to add to her recollections what she could make out of the present. She noticed that the Leighs scarcely ever spoke of Hamlin; that they brought in his flowers, books, and messages with a certain constraint, even, she thought, with an occasional look of disgust and indignation. And they never, never once mentioned Madame Elaguine.

"What has become of Sacha Elaguine?" she asked one day, rolling her head, with face even paler than before, and black crisp hair just beginning to cluster after cropping short, on the pillows. "Has she gone out of town? You have never spoken about her, Mary."

Mary Leigh, who was seated, holding Anne's thin white hand, did not raise her head; and Marjory, who was pouring out the tea hard by, flushed scarlet.

"Haven't I? Oh yes, I must," answered Mary Leigh, still keeping her eyes on the pattern of the carpet. "Madame Elaguine? Oh, she's just as usual."

"Odious little brute," scowled Marjory.

Mary raised her head sharply, and gave her sister a look of reproof.

Anne asked no more. She had understood: during her illness Sacha had tightened her hold on Hamlin; the Leighs had seen it, or been told, and Mary was afraid lest her sister should let out to the invalid what she imagined to be a heart-breaking secret.

"I am free!" thought Anne; and repeated these words to herself every time that one of the Leighs spoke coldly of Hamlin, or looked savage when he was mentioned. And sometimes she fancied that she could distinguish in the face and manner of the true-hearted Mary, of the indignant Marjory, the pain and perplexity of foreseeing that they possessed a terrible secret, that they must make a terrible revelation. Once, she felt sure, Mary's heart had almost burst for her silence. Miss Leigh had brought in Hamlin's usual gift of flowers, a bunch of beautiful white roses and jasmine; she was going to hand it to Anne, when her face suddenly contracted, and she stuffed the flowers roughly into a jar.

"Won't you let me smell Mr Hamlin's flowers, Mary?" asked Anne from her bed.

Mary Leigh gave her a long strange look.

"They aren't fit for you, Anne," said Mary, in a hoarse voice; "they're horrible, morbid sort of things—they'll just make your head ache."

"My head is much stronger than you think," said Anne; "let me have them—they are lovely. The jasmine doesn't smell like ordinary jasmine. What is it?—it smells like the incense that Sacha Elaguine burns in her boudoir; it's nice, but too strong. I wonder whether they have been in her boudoir to catch it. It's very kind of Mr Hamlin to bring them to me, especially as"—Anne looked up with a smile which frightened Mary Leigh out of her wits—"he doesn't care a bit about me any longer, you know."

Mary Leigh threw herself on her knees before Anne's bed, and drawing her head to her, kissed her.

"Oh, Annie, Annie, my darling!" she cried.

"You are good," answered Anne—"you are good to love me so. But Mr Hamlin is also very good, although he doesn't love me. I am very happy—so happy, Mary dear."

"She is mad," thought Mary, in terror, as Anne threw her head back, smiling, her onyx-grey eyes beaming, on the pillow. And she resolved that, as long as she could help, Anne Brown should not know what she knew, and what, every time that Hamlin's name was mentioned, sickened her heart.

Some days later Miss Brown was sufficiently well to exchange her bed for a couch in the drawing-room down-stairs; and then Hamlin asked whether he might be admitted to see her for a few minutes. He seemed painfully impressed at the sight of Anne, whom he was accustomed to see looking the embodiment of physical strength, a sort of primeval warrior-woman, stretched out on the sofa, so thin and hollow-checked, so pale, with a pallor quite different from the natural opaque ivory pallor of her complexion; so weak of voice and gesture, so wholly despoiled, it seemed to him, of her usual sombre haughtiness: resigned, and with the gentleness of a sick child. He was silent and depressed, as a man might be who knew her to be more seriously ill than she thought; and yet, as Anne was well aware, it was most obvious to him and to every one that she was entirely out of danger, and rapidly recovering. Miss Brown understood: he was weighed down, but with a worse conscience than Mary Leigh,—by the thought that this woman was unaware of the sort of treachery which was being committed behind her back. Anne, on the other hand, felt more really pleased to see him than she had done this long time past; it seemed as if, now that the bond which tied her to him was loosened, she could see once more all that was amiable and noble in him,—that she could like him again, feel towards him simply, naturally, as towards a friend and benefactor. And she felt sorry for his depression, for what she imagined to be his self-reproach; desirous of telling him almost, then and there, that he need not make himself unhappy, that he was free to love his cousin.

Miss Brown was still unfit for much conversation; and Hamlin seemed glad to cut short the interview. She asked him to raise one of the blinds; and when the light streamed upon his face, she thought she saw in it something unusual, something beyond his mere usual melancholy, a lassitude and look of being worried; again she felt sorry for him.

"How is your cousin Sacha?" she asked.

"She is well," he answered briefly, "and —sends you many messages. I don't let her come, because she would excite you. Goodbye."

Every afternoon Hamlin returned for a short time. Anne's first impression was merely strengthened; Hamlin was extraordinarily depressed, worried-looking, taciturn. Anne felt really sorry for him; he was evidently, she thought, eating his heart out in doubts and self-reproach; he had gone too far with Sacha to retreat, and yet his engagement to Miss Brown forbade his taking a decisive step. After all, he was truer and nobler than she had thought, more of her real Hamlin of former days; she reflected that this hostility of temperament and aims between them, this long and sickening endurance of a bond which suited neither, had made her unjust and bitter towards him, prone to seek for only his worse sides, neglectful of his good ones. She felt that it was not the least benefit of her release that she could now be perfectly grateful once more; that she could give to this man the affection which he really deserved, and which she really felt, now that the terrible debt of love was cancelled. She was sorry, very sorry for him, and determined that, since he had not the heart, it was for her to speak. But invariably, and as if warned by a secret intuition, he had interrupted the conversation, and gone away whenever she had been on the point of speaking. The bare name of Madame Elaguine seemed enough to send him away; and yet, whenever Anne succeeded in making him speak of his cousin, he had spoken of her with a strange bitterness, and almost disgust.

"He is mean, after all," thought Anne; "he is angry with poor Sacha for being the cause of his finding himself in a false position." And she determined that she would speak, not to him but to Madame Elaguine; she felt that she could not endure the way in which he would assuredly seek to whitewash himself at his cousin's expense. Mean, very mean; nay, something more than mean. What irritation or hypocrisy could induce him to speak of the woman whom he loved with a sort of constant innuendo, a constant sort of undercurrent of disgust?

And again she began to despise and dislike him. Another thing soon struck her. There was something unusual about Hamlin's appearance. Somewhat effeminate he had always been in his aristocratic refinement; but now it seemed to her as if there were in his face a something, half physical, half spiritual, a vague, helpless, half-stupefied look, which made her think of that hysterical tippling little poet Dennistoun, whom she disliked so much. Her mind reverted to what she had heard about Edmund Lewis having, at one period, induced Hamlin to take opium.

"Is Mr Lewis back?" she asked.

Hamlin flushed all over.

"Lewis is not likely to return," he answered briefly.

What was the meaning of it all? Hamlin was also, she noticed, no longer as careful in his dress as he had formerly been; there was something vaguely rowdy about him. And once, as he stooped over her to rearrange the cushions under her head, it seemed to her—was it true or not?—that she felt a sickening whiff, like those which she well remembered since her childhood, when her father had come in from drinking and taken her on his knees.

Was it possible that Hamlin, weak as he was, and feeling himself cornered in a false position, had taken to drinking—to drinking, which had been the fatal vice of his family, of his brother, father, and of his uncles, in order to rid himself of his worries?

She must speak to Madame Elaguine. She must let them know that they were free.

CHAPTER III.

WHILE she was in this perplexity about Hamlin, Miss Brown received a visit from her cousin Dick. She had scarcely seen him, and never alone, since that memorable walk home from Professor Richmond's lecture. Whether from the sense that he had gone too far, that his violence had offended and frightened her; or whether, more probably, from his having rushed to the conclusion that she was unattainable and perhaps unworthy of his seeking, Richard Brown had kept studiously out of her way.

For the first time in his life he came in with hesitation and almost shyness. He sat down by the side of her arm-chair, and spoke with a gentleness, a courtesy, that were quite unusual in him, and had a charm just from their contrast with his downright and gruff personality. The conversation rolled upon various indifferent subjects; he seemed to be feeling his way to something, trying to decide whether she was strong enough to admit of his saying something which weighed on his mind.

"You are nearly recovered now?" he asked. "Do you feel as if you were getting your strength back, Anne?"

"Oh yes," she answered; "I feel wonderfully well. I have been for a drive these last few days, and I am sure I could walk, if only they would let me. I only feel very tired and lazy every now and then."

There was a pause.

"Do you remember what you told me that afternoon when we walked home from Richmond's lecture—a rainy day at the end of March?" he asked suddenly.

"Yes, I do."

"You said, if you remember, that you did not care for Mr Hamlin, and that you felt yourself bound to him only by gratitude and the sense that he wanted you—do you remember, Nan?"

"I remember perfectly. Well?"

Richard Brown had spoken slowly and watching her face; and he seemed surprised at the perfect calm which he read in it.

"Well, I think it is right that you should know what is by this time known by all your acquaintances. Walter Hamlin no longer wants you; he has entirely thrown you over for another woman. He is—I don't know exactly what to call it, and don't mean any innuendo—well—the accepted lover of Madame Elaguine."

Anne nodded.

"I know it," she answered coolly. "I have known it, or at least guessed it, since a long while."

Richard was surprised, and, unconsciously perhaps to himself, mortified. He had always resented his cousin's fidelity to Hamlin, had always, with his tendency to seek for base motives wherever he could not sympathise, suspected that this fidelity was a mere cover for an unworthy love of the fine æsthetic gentleman or for his fortune and position; and he had anticipated a certain pleasure in seeing Anne wince beneath his revelation.

"It is no business of mine to pass a judgment over Mr Hamlin," he proceeded slowly, and wondering, suspicious as he always was with women, of the genuineness of Anne's imperturbability; "the whole business seems to me quite consonant with all my notions of his character."

"I do not think Mr Hamlin has acted dishonourably towards me," put in Anne, quietly; "on the contrary, I feel sure that he reproaches himself much more than he need."

"Very likely. What I was going to say is merely that this new turn which matters have taken necessarily implies an entire change in your position towards Mr Hamlin. He no longer wants you; you are therefore free. Am I correct in my view of the case?"

He was speaking with a deference to her opinion quite new in him.

"As far as I can judge," answered Anne, playing with a big lapis–lazuli rosary which she had taken off her neck, "I think you are quite correct, Dick. I believe I am free."

She hesitated and spoke the last words almost inaudibly, as if superstitiously afraid that they should be heard.

"In that case I presume you will have to remodel your life. Have you thought of any plans?"

"I have thought over the matter a good deal. My intention, as soon as Mr Hamlin and I have come to an explanation, which will be shortly, is to go to Ireland for a few months with Mary Leigh, to finish getting well and to finish some preparatory work, and then to go up to Girton. I should be able to pass the entrance examination in another three months. You see," she added, "Mr Hamlin, in spending the money that he has in turning me into a lady, has made it difficult for me to take to any such livelihood as would have naturally been mine under other circumstances; and I think, therefore, that I have a right to invest a portion of the money which he has settled upon me, and which he fully intended me to keep in any ease, in qualifying myself for the only sort of business for which I am now fit. He has settled upon me the equivalent of five hundred a–year, apart from the expenses of this house, of which I know nothing. Much less than that would more than cover the expenses of keeping me at Girton and of starting me as a teacher or journalist; and once fairly started, I hope I should be able to support myself and gradually to refund this money. Do you think that would be fair, Dick? You see, it is quite useless for me to think of ever repaying, even if money could repay in such matters, what Mr Hamlin has spent upon me during all these years."

She seemed to hesitate, to be afraid of being mean, of appearing to take advantage of Hamlin's generosity.

"Do you really contemplate renouncing the fortune which Mr Hamlin settled on you? giving up all the luxury to which he has accustomed you, Annie?"

Richard Brown, disinterested though he was, was too deeply impressed with the mercenary temper of mankind, to believe very easily in such sentiments.

"Why, of course," answered Anne. "When Mr Hamlin marries his cousin, he will find, that he has not too much with all his money. And I would certainly not keep any of it as soon as I could do without; though heaven knows I am not ungrateful, nor so silly as to fancy that I should be in the very least lightening my obligation towards him."

Richard did not answer for a moment. "Listen," he said, not without hesitation "I am nearer to you than Walter Hamlin and whatever I am, I owe it to your father. I find I have just made a very consider able and quite unexpected profit off some mining shares which Mr Gillespie left me. Let me advance you out of this money whatever may be wanted to defray your expenses at college; you will repay me when you find it convenient. In this way, you will be entirely independent of Mr Hamlin at once: you can let him have all his money."

Richard Brown hesitated, in a way very singular in his cut-and-dry nature; he seemed prepared for a rebuff.

"You are very kind, Dick; but I can't accept your offer. I owe it to Mr Hamlin, in return for all the generosity he has shown towards me and would still show, that I should never accept anything from any man but him, even if I were not resolved never to put myself under such an obligation again. I have no right to prefer your generosity to his."

Richard Brown was silent. Then, after a moment, they fell to talking about the plans and theories which occupied Cousin Dick's mind. He was unusually gentle and modest; he really seemed to be losing some of that narrowness which had been the ugly side of his powerful and upright nature.

"You are becoming quite tolerant, Dick," remarked Anne. "Six months ago you could never have conceived that any one unlike yourself or differing from your views could have anything good in him. I am very glad; it will make you more hopeful of the world, and show you a lot of energy and good faith which deserves to be united to your own, and which you would formerly have thrown upon the dust-heap."

"You are right," answered Brown. "I feel that I have diminished my own usefulness by not admitting any other kind of usefulness than my own. I often catch myself thinking, now, that my great danger lies in my tendency to underrate people; sometimes it seems as if, unless I can struggle against it, it will invade and sterilise my whole nature."

"I am so glad you feel like that, Dick."

"And do you know," he continued, "I think this change is due to you; knowing you has shown me how horribly unreasonable and unjust I am apt to be in my preconceived notions. I really did think you an æsthete once, Annie; nay, at one time, I was so base as to think that you were base, that you cared for Hamlin's position and money and good looks, while not caring for him. Will you forgive me, Annie?"

He bent over her, and took her hand. She let him hold it for a minute. She felt so strangely free, so safe, so happy somehow with this man, whose presence had so often been a threat and an insult.

"I wonder whether you will ever learn to be just to Mr Hamlin," she mused.

"I will do my best."

She had withdrawn her hand from his.

"I wonder whether I have ever been just to Mr Hamlin," said Anne.

Richard reddened.

"What makes you say that, Nan?"

"I don't know. I feel how difficult it is for a nature like mine to be just towards, to understand, any one outside it."

"Can you be just towards me?" he suddenly asked.

"I am, I think."

"Do you think, then," went on Richard Brown, "that during the time you spend at Girton you could try a little and understand me,—you could try and like me a little, Annie?"

"I do like you, Richard," she answered coldly; but a quiet happiness, like that of a windless, half-covered morning in the fields, stole over her.

"I don't mean this," he said, rising. "I want you to like me, Nan, as much—as much as you thought you liked Walter Hamlin."

Anne shook her head sadly.

"That is quite impossible," she said: "one doesn't feel like that twice, I fancy, Richard, any more than one believes twice in angels or such things."

Richard Brown frowned. She could never pluck Hamlin, Hamlin in some shape, real or false, out of her heart.

"Good–bye," he said; "I fear I have tired you. Annie," he added, "it is idiotic, isn't it? but all the time you were ill, even until I came into this room, I kept hoping that you might have lost your looks—that Hamlin might be quite unable ever to care for you again—that you might have ceased to be, in this sort of way, above me. And yet, when I saw you, I was glad it was not so. Oh, Nan, promise me you will try and like me a little."

"Please don't say that, Dick. I have been a slave, a prisoner. Can't you understand that my great joy is the sense of my freedom, my sense of belonging to no one, caring about no one? Can't you understand that it seems horrible to me to even think that I could ever care for any one again? Can't you let me enjoy my liberty, at least until I have realised that it isn't a dream?"

She spoke with impetuosity, but gently; and her cousin did not feel rebuked.

"By the way," he said, "I suppose you have heard who is expected here soon—your old friend, Melton Perry."

"Melton Perry!" cried Anne. It seemed such centuries since she had heard that name last. "Oh, I shall be so glad to see him, he is such a good man!"

She walked up and down after Dick had left.

Melton Perry! the name brought up the far, far distant past—a vision of the untidy house at Florence; of Mrs Perry's lean and Sapphic profile; of the tall grass and crushed herbs in the vineyard of the Villa Arnolfini; of Hamlin as she had first known him—a mysterious, unattainable ideal high above her; of the studio at the top of the tower; of herself, as she recollected herself to have been, a sombre, unhappy creature, with whose identity she seemed to have no connection, and into whose dark and confused mind she felt unable to see. There was something very painful in this sudden return of the past in company with her old friend, and Anne thought bitterly of the difference between the dreams of happiness, so positive, so perfect, of those days, and the reality of happiness, so negative, so poor—consisting in what? in being left to herself—which belonged to her now. And yet, after all, as she looked into her girlhood before Hamlin's coming, she recognised the same negativeness; she had wished to be free, to be a daily governess, to depend upon no one for her livelihood, to be able to know something of a wider life. She had never hoped, scarcely even wished, for happiness; the semblance of it had passed before her eyes, had, for a brief time, made her life more acutely sensitive; but she returned to the negative: it was the law of her life.

And, as she cleared her mind of all vain regrets, she became aware that, in a manner, this return upon her scene of Melton Perry was like the ringing of the bell, the orchestral flourish, which ends a piece as it has begun it. The comedy of her love for Hamlin, and of Hamlin's love for her, was over; and she felt impatient for Melton Perry's arrival.

CHAPTER IV.

THE day after this visit from Cousin Dick, came the first visit from Madame Elaguine. It seemed to Anne that, from the very moment of her entering the room, she could perceive something strange in Sacha's manner—something brazen, flaunting, cruel. The little woman somehow no longer looked so small and that childish appealingness had entirely left her manner; she was self-possessed, cynical, triumphant. Her very dress was different from anything in which Miss Brown had hitherto seen her; exotic indeed and fantastic, like everything that she wore, but certainly not turned out by Madame Elaguine's maid. She kissed Anne familiarly on both cheeks, enveloping her in an atmosphere of heady Eastern perfumes.

"Poor Annie," she said, "you have been very ill, and must have thought me a great brute for not coming to see you before. But Walter absolutely forbade my coming—stood in front of your door, so to speak, and shut it in my face. He pretended that I should have excited you too much. Perhaps I should; I am a wretched, excitable creature. Perhaps he was right; what do you think?" Madame Elaguine fixed her eyes on those of Anne; a long look of scrutiny and triumph, as if she had expected to see her wince.

"I think Mr Hamlin was quite mistaken," answered Miss Brown quietly, understanding the meaning of that look. "I am much less subject to excitement than he supposes; and your presence would not have excited me more than any one else's."

"Really!" and Madame Elaguine's mouth took a peculiar little sneering turn; "I should have thought that I *was* exciting, now. Not more exciting, for instance, than the Miss Leighs? or than your cousin, Mr Richard Brown?" and she again looked scrutinisingly at Anne, who merely shook her head. "By the way, your cousin has quite cut me of late, Annie—ask him why. I suspect that he thinks me a dangerous woman, quite without moral ballast,—what my German teacher used to call *Sittlicher Ernst*. He was such a funny creature that German teacher of mine; did I ever tell you about him? He taught at the school where I was in Petersburg: a thin lank creature, with long red wrists projecting a yard from his sleeves, and a waistcoat which would ride up whenever he was excited; he used to lean against the wall, any part of his body at random, and bend and sway the rest of him about, like a caterpillar. He taught us German literature, and was very shocked because I said the 'Bride of Corinth' was the only amusing thing Goethe had ever written. He believed in Schopenhauer—and hated women, and me in particular, because I had no *Sittlicher Ernst*; and one day, what do you think he did? he fell on his knees and tried to catch me round the waist. Poor devil! he was turned out of doors, and drowned himself later. I wonder whether it was out of despair at my want of *Sittlicher Ernst*? He was such a queer creature. I sometimes think, after all, he was the only man I could really have loved, if only his waistcoat had not ridden up, and his wrists projected so much from his cuffs."

Sacha laughed, and bit her lower lip a little, so that it suddenly became scarlet, like the lips of Edmund Lewis. She threw herself back in her chair, one foot crossed over the other, her eyes fixed on the Venetian chandelier, which caught opalescent lights in the sunshine; she was smiling, perhaps in recollection of the professor with his wrists and his waistcoat.

Anne did not know what to say; the presence of this woman seemed to freeze her, like the contact of some clammy thing: it was as if the soul of Edmund Lewis had entered her body and had become more active, more subtle in its new habitation. Mechanically her eyes rested upon Madame Elaguine's dress, a marvellous vague thing, made in some confused resemblance of the men's dress of Moliére's time,—a crimson plush coat and a big man's cravat of Flanders lace, but all bursting out, by every conceivable slashing and gap, into a mass of lace, which hung about her like a cloud of thistle–down, beneath which her thin and nervous little body seemed to twist and writhe with every word.

"It's a pretty frock, isn't it?" she remarked, looking down upon it with satisfaction. "Oh no, I didn't make this; I am bored with always making my own frocks. It's from Worth. I swore I would bring round Watty from belief in pre–Adamitic skirts and purfled sleeves and eighteen–penny medievalism to a belief in Worth; you know he used always to rant at Paris clothes. Well, I've been as good as my word; this is from Worth, and what's more, Walter has paid my bill. Humiliating, rather, isn't it? but then, you see, I'm a pauper, and can't buy Worth frocks on a thousand a–year, including subscription for a copy of Chough's new translation of 'Villon,' with all the improprieties annotated, Dutch paper, morocco, rough edges, price three guineas, can I?"

Anne flushed. Hamlin had paid for Sacha's dress! And yet, had Hamlin not paid for not merely one, but all Anne's dresses these years—nay, for everything that Anne saw about her—nay, for everything almost that Anne knew and was? And still, how was it, there was a difference? and as she looked at Sacha in her fantastic Molière coat of crimson plush and watered white silk and lace, which Hamlin had paid for, she could not get out of her mind the image of certain French kept women whom she had seen, in their elaborate dresses and well–appointed victorias, driving in the Park. It was very unjust and horrible, yet she could not get it out of her mind.

"Walter is a queer creature," went on Madame Elaguine; "somewhat like my Ger- man caterpillar professor: I don't mean in the matter of wrists and waistcoats, but in the matter of women. I don't know how to say it; my ideas aren't ever very clear: I suppose it's want of *Sittlicher Ernst*, and also because I'm hysterical—at least the doctors say so; because I insist on having my own way. I mean that Walter, for instance, hates me in a certain sense just as that professor did. I'm sure he sometimes feels as if he could throttle me, because I have no *Sittlicher Ernst*, and because I made love to him, and offered him barley–sugar and tops when I was ten. And yet! Ah, well, I suppose I am a wretch! Oh, Annie dear, I fear, I fear I am a wretch!" and Madame Elaguine suddenly jumped up from her chair and flung her arms round Miss Brown's neck and kissed her, with such violence that Anne felt her lips almost like leeches and her teeth pressing into her cheeks.

"Oh Annie, I am an unworthy wretch! I am a beast towards you!" she cried.

Anne felt a horror, a kind of fear of death; and yet she felt sorry for this woman; was she not a wretch in not clearing up the position—in letting this woman continue to love in shame, when she might love openly and honourably? She loosened herself from Sacha's embrace.

"Madame Elaguine" she began, feeling her face still burning from this strangling embrace, and mechanically smoothing her ruffled hair, "I have long wanted to tell you something with regard to Mr Hamlin—indeed I feel I ought to have told it you before, but . . ." At this moment the door opened and Hamlin entered.

Anne had missed her opportunity; it was impossible to speak before Hamlin, although she had once or twice contemplated clearing up matters to him and his cousin at the same time. But it was impossible now. Sacha had something strange, brazen, about her, which froze Anne's soul. Hamlin was listless, depressed, with that hang–dog, stupefied air that Miss Brown had noticed in him of late. He spoke little, barely answered any of Sacha's remarks: every time that he raised his eyes upon his cousin, it was with an expression that amounted almost to disgust; and she seemed nowise hurt, but rather amused and pleased at this look, and took a pleasure in provoking it by a hundred absurdities, and by a sort of bullying way, as if expressly to show her power over this sullen creature.

They did not stay long. Madame Elaguine rose, and Hamlin mechanically followed her example: was it that he could not see her go away by herself, or that he was afraid of being left alone with Miss Brown?

"This is my first visit to you since your illness, and it will be my last for a little time," said Madame Elaguine, letting Hamlin help her on with her cloak, and spinning out the operation, as if to show that this depressed and sullen creature, for all his sulkiness, was her slave.

"Are you going away?" cried Anne, a sudden fear entering her heart. Sacha no– ticed her involuntary flush, and mistook its meaning.

"Only for a fortnight," she answered, with an odd smile. "Oh no; I can't do without London and my friends—hideous London and disagreeable friends, at least so far as

Walter is concerned. I suppose it's my perversity and want of *Sittlicher Ernst*, again. I am going to Paris this evening. I have a notion of taking Boris out of his English school and sending him to the Lycée. I feel I have had a surfeit of respectability and æstheticism, and that I'd rather my son were a Frenchman and a Bohemian. It's a whim. Perhaps it will make me return a frantic Anglomaniac. Fancy if Boris were to grow up a thing like this!" pointing to Hamlin,—"a horrible pseudo Sir Galahad, as Watty was at sixteen. Faugh! I couldn't bear it. Good–bye, Annie dear; I fear you must think me an immoral woman, and that my German professor wasn't so far wrong. Good–bye, my beautiful Madonna of the Glaciers," and again Miss Brown was half stifled in the cloud of oriental perfumes, as Madame Elaguine kissed her cavalierly on both cheeks.

"Come along, Watty!" cried Sacha; "can't you learn to open the door for a woman?"

"Good–bye, Miss Brown," and Hamlin gave a little sigh of weariness as he pressed Anne's hand.

Miss Brown remained in a state of vague fear all that day. Was that love—at least on Hamlin's part—that look of bored disgust with which he had responded to Madame Elaguine's provocation? Anne grew pale at the notion of that fortnight of Sacha's absence. Would Hamlin, fickle, easily wounded in his vanity, sated with Madame Elaguine's Russian ways, remain faithful to the absent woman? Would he not rather return and begin afresh that old, old story of Platonic adoration, of self–reproach, with what his cousin called Madonna of the Glaciers? And as Hamlin was leaving, he had said to her half audibly, "If you will allow me, I will come to–morrow afternoon and see what can be done to my Vision of Beatrice, if you will give me a sitting."

A sitting! Anne's heart had sunk at the mere word.

But the next morning she found on the tray on which her breakfast was brought up a twisted note. It was from Hamlin, written late the previous night.

"DEAR MISS BROWN," it said,—"I fear you will think me very uncourteous to break through our engagement for to–morrow morning. But I am feeling rather anxious lest Madame Elaguine should get imposed on about the school for her boy; so I shall join her for a few days in Paris. Pray forgive my apparent rudeness.—Yours sincerely, W. H."

"What's your news, Annie?" asked Mary Leigh, who had come in to see after her invalid. "You look as if you had come in for a fortune!"

Anne made an effort and laughed.

"It was only Mr Hamlin postponing a sitting which I was to give him. I really don't feel much like sitting yet. Mr Hamlin's gone to Paris to look after a school for Boris Elaguine."

"And Madame Elaguine?"

"Madame Elaguine—went yesterday."

"Oh, indeed!" answered Mary Leigh; and as she said that, a wave of red came into Miss Brown's pale face—why, Anne could not herself have explained.

CHAPTER V.

THE day after Hamlin's departure to join Madame Elaguine, Richard Brown paid another visit at Hammersmith; and he dropped in frequently in the next few days. He never spoke of his hopes, he never inquired about Anne's plans; he scarcely so much as alluded to Hamlin's departure. He seemed satisfied to see his cousin, to explain to her all the things that he hoped some day to do. This forbearance, this delicate discretion, on the part of one of the most tactless and exacting of men; this something which implied that Cousin Dick had learned to consult her wishes, touched Miss Brown very much. Love, or by whatever other name (since the name of love was discredited to Anne) she might choose to call Richard's strong and steady feeling, seemed to have purified this powerful and generous temper of that alloy of coarse and contemptuous suspicion that had occasionally repelled her so much.

Richard Brown had become comparatively quite charitable in his judgments, sincerely anxious to be just. He tried to see things a little from her point of view—nay, even to understand whatever good there was or had been in Hamlin. This big and self-reliant man, who had already thought and done so much for himself and for others, began to appear to his cousin as less mature than she had fancied, and even less self-reliant; new instincts and perceptions, new sides of his nature—making it fuller, richer, purer—developing under her influence. Anne did not love her cousin; she did not even anticipate loving him anything as she had once loved Hamlin. She recognised that, in her nature, love could exist only for an ideal, and in an ideal she could never again believe; but she became aware of a relation of frank comradeship, of mutual respect and attachment and usefulness, which warmed her nature, and made hopes and projects bud and blossom up. She was nervously anxious for that fortnight to have come to an end, to have Hamlin back, to speak to him; and yet, at the same time, it seemed to her dreadful that these few days of freedom from care, freedom from the shadow which had so long hung over her, should so soon come to an end.

The fortnight was drawing to a close; Hamlin would soon be back. Anne began to be filled with unendurable impatience; she even, once or twice, began a letter telling him everything, and tore it up only from the fear that it might seem harsh, ungrateful, that it might (and the idea was terrible to her) make him suppose that she was jealous, that she loved him. It was a great relief to her when there suddenly came a telegram, sent on from Hamlin's lodgings, and opened by his servant, which announced for next evening the arrival of Melton Perry, who knew nothing of Hamlin's momentary absence from town.

"Oh, Aunt Claudia," cried Anne, "Mr Perry is coming to-morrow evening! Do you think—oh, do you think you could have him to stay here till Mr Hamlin return?"

"Who is Mr Perry?" asked Chough, who was dining with them, suddenly pricking up his ears at Anne's excited tone. Could *he* be the explanation of Anne's indifference to Hamlin? thought the poet of the Eternal Feminine.

"Mr Perry," answered Anne, "is the gentleman in whose house I was a servant until I met Mr Hamlin—the father of the little girls whose maid I was. He was very kind to me, and I am very fond of him."

Cosmo Chough stared at her in amazement. He had quite forgotten, indeed he had never properly realised, that this queenly woman, this more than Dante's Beatrice or Petrarch's Laura, had actually been a nursemaid—a servant! She a servant! he repeated to himself, looking at Miss Brown as she sat opposite him; at this goddess, it seemed to him, with the wonderful face as of one of Michelangelo's Titanesses; the solemn, mysterious, onyx−grey eyes; the something superhumanly grand in person and movement. To have been a servant, and to remind people of it, was his next thought; and this Cosmo Chough, conscious of his supposed father the duke, and of his real father the apothecary at Limerick, was absolutely unable to comprehend.

"Mr Perry, except Miss Curzon, was the only friend I ever had, until—until I met Mr Hamlin," went on Miss Brown. "You will give him the spare room, Aunt Claudia, for my sake, won't you? And you will let me arrange it for him, and make it look a little untidy, and put match−boxes and pipe−lights about, so that he may feel a little comfortable."

Mrs Macgregor laughed.

"Put as many pipe−lights about as you please, my dear; but if he fill Watty's studio with pipe−smoke, you will be responsible, not I."

The next afternoon Anne Brown was just in the midst of what she called making the spare room look untidy, taking out the superfluous æsthetic furniture which would, she knew, fidget her former master to death, dragging in leather arm−chairs instead of imitation Queen Anne things, and piling newspapers and novels on the table, when a visitor was announced. She went down into the drawing−room, and, to her surprise, found Edmund Lewis. An inexpressible sense of disgust came over her, This man personified all that she hated most of that past with which she was about to break for ever. The little man with the auburn beard and sealing−wax lips was considerably less free−and−easy and sultan−like than usual; his humiliation, whatever it was, had evidently done him good. Indeed, Miss Brown was almost beginning to ask herself whether she might not have been a little unjust towards him also, so respectful and amiable had he made himself, when it began to dawn upon her that there was an explanation for his visit much more in keeping with the character she had hitherto attributed to him.

"I hear that Walter Hamlin is in Paris with his cousin," he had remarked, after a few minutes' conversation. He had tried to say it in an off−hand manner; but Anne had felt his green eyes fixed curiously upon her.

"Yes; they have gone to settle about sending Boris to the Lycée."

Lewis hereupon made some remarks about English and French schools, and upon the education of Boris Elaguine; but slowly and dexterously he made the conversation return to Sacha and Hamlin; he made the conspicuous matter no longer the object of Madame Elaguine's and Hamlin's journey to Paris, but the journey itself.

"I don't think Madame Elaguine's Russian relations—her aunt who lives in Paris and Boris's grandfather—will be particularly pleased at her going about like that with a young man," he said. "Russians are such corrupt people, they see mischief in everything."

Anne understood. Edmund Lewis, who always hated her, had been unable to resist the temptation, now that both Hamlin and Sacha were safe out of the way, of seeing the proud Miss Brown wince beneath his compassion. He was artistically playing upon the feelings of humiliation and anger with which he imagined her to be filled.

"Madame Elaguine is Mr Hamlin's cousin, you must remember," answered Anne, quietly bending over her embroidery.

"True; but the people who meet them in Paris won't know that, or won't believe it. Besides, it's not as if they had always lived together and been as brother and sister, as some cousins have. I think Madame Elaguine is very rash to run the risk of unnecessary gossip; and I must say I can't understand Hamlin being so dense as not to see that he was compromising his cousin, especially as people were beginning to notice his assiduity to his cousin even here. Of course, however," added Lewis, fixing his eyes on Miss Brown, "being engaged, to you makes a difference to Hamlin. A man who is engaged to be married may, I suppose, go about with any woman—it is as if he were married. I am very sorry I shall be far away, somewhere in Central Asia or South America—I don't know where—when your marriage will come off, Miss Brown. I must make my congratulations betimes."

"There is nothing to congratulate about," answered Anne, quietly; "there has been no question of my marrying Mr Hamlin. I am sorry such an idea should have got abroad. I was, you know, Mr Hamlin's ward till lately, and I am now taking advantage of his aunt's kindness to stay here till—till I settle what I am going to do; I may be going to Girton—I don't know."

"Oh, indeed!" exclaimed Lewis; "pray forgive my unintentional impertinence then. Girton? Ah—How long do you intend remaining there?"

"I don't know. Nothing is settled yet." Anne was determined not to let this man enjoy his impertinence and spitefulness: he should go away baffled.

"I may stay there altogether. I should rather like to be a teacher."

"And I," said Lewis, with one of his would-be fascinating smiles, "would, in that case, like to be a pupil, Miss Brown."

Anne did not answer. He must be disappointed, she thought. But he was determined to get some satisfaction out of her.

"I can't get over Hamlin's thoughtlessness in accompanying Madame Elaguine to Paris," he said. "It would have been so simple to ask some lady to be of the party. I suppose you did not like leaving Mrs Macgregor? I was sorry to hear that she was ailing."

"There was no question of my going," answered Anne; "and I do think it is such silly nonsense about any one being required. If people choose to think that Mr Hamlin is going to marry his cousin—well, why not? It would be a very natural thing if he did."

She looked Lewis boldly in the face. It was the first time that she had said the thing which she believed, hoped for, prayed for.

Edmund Lewis was evidently staggered; and Anne enjoyed watching his discomfiture. But a thought soon came into his subtle head.

"I suppose you see a good deal of Mr Richard Brown?" he asked; "he's an extraordinarily clever man."

"Yes; he is very able. I see him often enough. At present his electioneering business doesn't leave him much time."

"Ah, to be sure. It costs a lot of money, doesn't it, to get into Parliament? But I suppose Mr Brown is rich now, is he not?"

"He is well off."

"And he is sure to succeed. He has a fine career before him," mused Lewis. He had, as he thought, grasped the situation: there had been an amicable exchange—Anne was to marry Richard Brown, and Sacha was to have Hamlin. All his enemies—for Sacha and Hamlin had evidently sent him to the right- about—were going to be happily settled. His paste-coloured face grew pastier than ever; he bit his scarlet lips and auburn moustache; he looked horribly angry and malignant; wickeder than even Anne, who had always hated him, would have believed it possible.

But he kept his temper—nay, he was quite unusually deferential and sweet. He led the conversation to other topics; and Anne thought that his only object was now to talk no more about the affairs which he had so misjudged, when, she scarcely knew how, he began to talk about Wotton Hall—first about the scenery, then about the grounds, then the house, then their stay there, and finally about the incident of the burning bed.

He went over all the circumstances of it; he summed up all that he and Anne knew of Madame Elaguine's persecution; and then, as if discussing a curious psychological problem, he asked her whether it had ever occurred to her that there was any possibility that the persecution should be a fraud, and that the bed had been set fire to by Madame Elaguine herself. "I don't know whether you remarked at the time, that the flames burst out just two minutes after Madame Elaguine had fetched the cigarette-papers out of her room, and that she had given orders to her maid not to come until she should be rung for," said Lewis; "also, that Madame Elaguine seemed extremely unwilling that any inquiry should be made into the matter afterwards."

Anne said nothing; the recollection of the precious lace-trimmed dressing-gown, placed carefully out of the way of the flames, and of that sentence, "And they never forgot, so long as they lived, that terrible burning bed," which had caught her eye in little Hélène Elaguine's story-book, came into her mind. She had put that matter of the persecution behind her of late, and yet in her heart she felt that she believed it to be a fraud.

"I have had my doubts about it," bending over her work lest Lewis should see her face. "Indeed," she added boldly, indignant at her own want of frankness, "I am inclined to believe that Madame Elaguine did set that bed on fire. Several things have made me think so."

Lewis smiled. "I am glad to find that you take my view of the case, Miss Brown. The chemist at Appledore—where, if you remember, Madame Elaguine went for some shopping the day before the fire—showed me himself the bottle of acid from which he had helped Madame Elaguine—I forget the name of the stuff—she said she wanted some to take spots out of a dress."

"Indeed," went on Lewis, "I think that we have in Madame Elaguine a very curious instance of a sort of monomania which has, I believe, its scientific name,"—and Lewis began to retail a variety of instances, culled out of some volume of 'Causes célèbres,' of persons who had elaborately made up persecutions of which themselves were victims. He had always been fond of talking as if he knew a great deal about morbid conditions of the brain, and, indeed, morbid things of all sorts; and he talked for some time as if he took a purely abstract interest in the case.

"One is apt to meet very singular types among Russian women, especially such as have led a wandering life like Madame Elaguine," went on Lewis. "They are devoured by a passion for the forbidden, or at least for the unreal and theatrical; there is something strangely crooked in their moral vision, something discordant in their nature. They are extraordinary, charming, intelligent, depraved creatures. Only a Russian woman could be at once so childish and so theatrical and insincere, so full of idealism and of cynicism, as Madame Elaguine. Ah, she is a wonderful being! That matter of the burning bed finishes her off perfectly."

Edmund Lewis fixed his green magnetic eyes on Anne. He still believed that she must hate Sacha, as it was clear that, for some reason or other, he hated the Russian; and he wished, by giving Miss Brown these notions about Madame Elaguine, to induce her to revenge herself and him. But Anne had become quite dense to his intentions. She did not connect these ideas with Lewis; his words seemed to her now the mere expression of all the things which her own instinct had revealed, and which she had put behind her in her desire that Sacha should relieve her of the intolerable debt to Hamlin. The creature described by this odious man was the real Sacha; she was Madame Elaguine as she now clearly appeared to Miss Brown. And yet how unjust! Lewis had wanted to torment her by making her jealous of Madame Elaguine; he now wished to pay off Madame Elaguine for having, in some manner, slighted his own vanity.

"I think you take a dreadful view of the matter," she said; "you explain Madame Elaguine, who is only half a Russian, by all the horrible Russians you have ever met or imagined. I think there is a much simpler explanation. Madame Elaguine has been very strangely brought up; she has lived with very bad people; her husband was a horrible wretch, we all know. She is excessively hysterical—her mother, Mr Hamlin's aunt, was so also—and we all know that the desire to be prominent, to deceive, is a common form of hysteria. And as she has never been brought up to restrain herself, she imagines herself to be persecuted, and makes up the persecution. She is much more to be pitied than to be blamed."

Anne spoke rapidly. She seemed to be speaking fairly; and yet she knew she was wilfully misrepresenting, that Madame Elaguine was something more than a hysterical monomaniac: she remembered Mrs Macgregor's stories of Sacha's degraded childhood, all the accusations of her precocious lying and unchastity, of her having led one of her cousins into mischief, and set the house by the ears. She was indignant with herself for defending this woman—out of charity? out of conviction? No. But merely because she required that this woman be sufficiently innocent to become Hamlin's wife.

Edmund Lewis stroked his auburn beard meditatively.

"I don't believe in praise and blame," he answered; "I believe merely in fate. Some people are born noble, truthful, chaste—others just the reverse. It is the fault of neither; and each, in its way, is equally interesting and valuable to the artist or the psychologist. The curious thing about Madame Elaguine is, that she apparently stands half-way; she is, according to the ideas of the world, half responsible and half irresponsible. We see in her a hysterical woman, troubled by a morbid love of deceit; and at the same time a woman to whom such deceit is or has been practically necessary. Madame Elaguine continues for her amusement, and develops to the utmost, an imaginary persecution, whose origin must be sought in some intrigue which it was her interest to veil by a mystification," Lewis drawled on in his omniscient, half-pedantic way, as if the intrigues of married women were the most usual subject of conversation between a man and a young lady, and as if to suggest that Madame Elaguine had led a loose life were the most obvious and inoffensive of proceedings.

Miss Brown blushed crimson; but she felt something more than insulted, something more than indignant. What right had this man to focus all her own suspicions concerning a woman whom she fervently wished not to suspect?

"Mr Lewis," she said, "I don't think those things should be listened to by me or said by you. I believe that Madame Elaguine is not sound in her mind, and that her persecution is a hoax; but I believe that she is an honest woman in other respects. She is a friend of mine, and I will not hear her slandered."

"Heaven forbid that I should wish to slander her! I think she is a fascinating woman; and she is—at least she was—quite as great a friend of mine as of yours. I was only telling you how I explain her character."

Lewis had always appeared a reptile in Anne's eyes; but never so much as just now.

"I hate scandal," he said, taking his hat, "and I am most grieved to have appeared to be talking scandal. People always misunderstand the sort of passionate interest I take in every kind of curious character. I suppose you would call it morbid, Miss Brown; but I really was considering Madame Elaguine merely as an interesting study."

All this kind of talk, of which Hamlin was so fond, perfectly sickened Anne; and the sudden stirring up of all her old suspicions was exasperating.

"That is all very fine," she said angrily; "but do you, or do you not, believe Madame Elaguine to be a dishonourable woman, apart from this monomania?"

"It is very hard to say. You know I disbelieve in what you call moral responsibilities. I imagine Madame Elaguine to have found her mania for persecution very convenient at one period of her life—yes, cer– tainly. I think it is the only rational way to account for the beginning of it—don't you?"

Miss Brown took no notice of Lewis's insolent inquisitiveness of manner.

"If you think that, Mr Lewis," she said, "may I ask how you reconciled with your notions of gentlemanly behaviour the calm way in which you let Mr Hamlin introduce such a woman as you describe to me, and let me continue to know her? No; you are perfectly aware that all this is merely trumped up at the moment." And she put her hand on the bell–handle, for the door to be opened to Lewis.

Edmund Lewis smiled.

"Walter Hamlin's eyes are quite as good as mine. As regards my behaviour towards you, I cannot go into details, but you may understand, dear Miss Brown, that two or three months ago I may not, as a man of honour, have been at liberty to discuss Madame Elaguine's character in the way that I have done now that Madame Elaguine's relations with me have entirely changed their nature. Good-bye, dear Miss Brown. I am most truly grieved if I have offended you in any way."

Anne merely made an impatient gesture, a gesture almost of disgust, as Edmund Lewis left the room.

So this was the explanation of Edmund Lewis's apparent disgrace! Sacha Elaguine had repelled his odious advances, she had closed her door to him, she had complained to Hamlin; and now, as soon as their backs were turned, Lewis had come to slander them without fear of a horsewhipping. Anne seemed to breathe once more—thank heaven that the wretch had overreached himself in his malice!

CHAPTER VI.

THE door had scarcely closed upon Edmund Lewis, when it opened again suddenly.

"Mr Perry!" cried Anne, rising and running forward as a child might run to meet a former kind and encouraging teacher; "Mr Perry! oh I am so glad to see you!"

It really seemed to her that this dear, good, open familiar face, with the untidy yellow hair and beard,—that this well-known, boyish, slouching figure drove away like some cabalistic sign the loathsome creature who had been there a few minutes before,—that Melton Perry dispelled all the horrid vision left behind by Edmund Lewis.

"Didn't expect me yet, eh, Annie—I mean Miss Brown?" said Melton Perry, as she seized his hand in both hers. "I suppose you expected me by the Dover train. But I came by

Dieppe, six hours' agony, but a saving of twelve-and-sixpence. I was always an economical creature, wasn't I? Why, what's that you have round your neck? That beastly little pewter and horn rosary that I got you at the Fair of the Impruneta, by George! Fancy your having kept such a thing!"

"It's one of the best things I have," said Anne, the tears coming into her eyes as this well-known voice brought back the far-distant past—"it's the present of a friend."

"And all this, isn't this also the present of a friend?" said Perry, throwing himself into an arm-chair, and looking round the room with much the same wonder with which Anne had looked at its strange furniture, its brocades and embroideries, and Japanese vases and lustre plates, when she first came; "but I forgot, Walter Hamlin isn't a particular friend of yours."

To this jest Miss Brown made no answer: if only Melton Perry could guess at the literal truth of his words!

"Lord, what a damned gorgeous place this is!" cried Perry, still looking round; and then, suddenly turning towards Anne, where she sat, in a wonderful trailing dress of deep crimson stamped velvet, a big bunch of blackish crimson roses marking off, throwing into relief, the strange opaque ivory of her face, "what a beautiful woman you are, Annie! Do you know, I usen't to believe it, when Watty raved about you at the Villa Arnolfini. What a crusty old jackass I must have been! But tell, why in the wide world aren't you married yet? What have you been doing all this time?"

"Mr Hamlin has not asked me to marry him yet," answered Anne, laconically.

Melton Perry thrust his hands upon the arms of his chair, and his whole body forward. "Not asked you to marry him yet!" he repeated; "do you mean to say you aren't engaged to him . . .?"

Anne shook her head.

"That he's been going loafing, and spooning, and doing *Vita Nuova* all this time? I thought that he must have lost two dozen grandfathers and grandmothers in rapid succession, so that one mourning postponed your marriage after the other, or something similar." Then a thought suddenly struck him. "Hamlin's not ill?" he cried. "Consumption, madness, doctors' consultations,—anything of that sort?"

Miss Brown could not help smiling.

"Oh no, Mr Hamlin has been quite well. He is in Paris at present; he didn't expect you quite so soon, but he will be back in a day or two."

Melton Perry rose and looked Anne very earnestly in the face—

"Miss Brown—no, I can't call you Miss Brown—Annie, tell me the truth. Has Hamlin not kept his word—has he played you any dirty trick? No, no, I don't mean anything,—but, has Hamlin played fast and loose with you?"

"Mr Hamlin never intended asking me to marry him at once," answered Anne, evasively. She felt in Melton Perry's suspicions that again, as with her cousin, Hamlin would be attacked, maligned, that she would have to defend him. "Don't you remember, Mr Perry? We were to wait, to see whether we really . . . I will tell you all about it later—to-morrow. It is a long story; I want to hear about you now, about Italy—about your work, the children, Mrs Perry."

"Mr Hamlin," she added, fearing lest her evasive answers, her haste to get rid of the subject, should prejudice Perry against his friend, "has been most generous and noble towards me; indeed much more than I can ever say."

"I'm damned if I understand any of it," said Perry to himself, as he proceeded to answer Anne's rapid strings of questions about his wife, his little girls, his pictures, his etchings,—those etchings, never thought of before, which had revealed in this sixth-rate painter a great artist, and had brought him, in good case to make money, to England. Miss Brown insisted upon showing him up to his room herself. As she was leaving him, he looked at her long and seriously.

"Annie," he said, "if it's not rude to ask, for I've forgotten—how old are you?"

"I was twenty-four last month. Why do you ask? Do you think I look more?"—she added, with a smile whose bitterness he did not catch. She could scarcely realise it herself; she seemed to have lived so long, such years and years since she had seen him last—nay, since she had first entered this room.

"Twenty-four," repeated Perry, stupidly. "Well now, don't be offended—of course you couldn't be more, for you weren't of age when you left us; but somehow—it isn't that you don't look young, you know, but all the same I should have thought . . . I'm a rude brute."

"That I was much older," laughed Miss Brown. "Well, I often think so myself."

"It's something, I don't know what. You are far handsomer than in Italy, and you never did look much like a girl—you know what I mean; but now, upon my word, I don't know how to say it, I never saw an unmarried woman look like you. You look as if you had seen and understood such a heap of things. I feel quite a fool before you. Forgive me," he said, "I'm always a blundering tomfool. I had somehow thought of you as something like my own girls. Winnie's sixteen, you know, and such a strapping girl. But I feel as if you might be my grandmother."

Anne laughed. "I have always felt as if I were your grandmother. I was born old. Good-bye, Mr Perry. Remember that dinner is at seven; and put on a dress-coat if you want to win the heart of my aunt—I mean Mr Hamlin's aunt."

Melton Perry whistled as he stooped to unbuckle his portmanteau.

"I'm damned if I understand anything of it all, and Annie least of any of them," he mused.

CHAPTER VII.

"**AFTER** all," said Melton Perry to himself next morning, as he sat under the big apple-trees in the garden, smoking his pipe and looking at Miss Brown stitching at a piece of embroidery and overwhelming him with questions about Winnie, Mildred, Leila, the baby, Mrs Perry—nay, even about all her former fellow-servants in Italy, and the grocer round the corner, and the milkman, and the man who came from the country every

Monday to fetch the linen,—"after all, it was a very bright idea of old Watty's to fall in love with our nursemaid and turn her into a wonderful æsthetic being in a wonderful æsthetic house: it was very sensible of Mrs Perry to encourage him in the idea; and it was just like a confounded, fumbling, purblind old pig and ass like me to try and prevent it."

After lunch Anne took Melton Perry up into the drawing-room, cool, and almost Italian, with drawn blinds and a faint smell of flowers in the dusk, on one of the most stifling London afternoons. Perry mechanically took out a cigarette; but he hastily put it in again. It seemed to him profanation to smoke in such a wonderful room, in the presence of such a wonderful woman.

"Please smoke; you used always to smoke after lunch with Mrs Perry," said Anne.

"But—this isn't Florence; and you—you aren't Mrs Perry."

Anne made an impatient gesture that he should take out his cigarettes again. She had determined that she must speak to him before Hamlin came; that she must try and get him to understand, to explain things to Hamlin. But how get this good-natured, kindly, childish, yet in a way chivalrous, harum-scarum creature to understand her story? She had a great dread of the impossibility of making him understand that Hamlin had never acted meanly towards her—that their estrangement was due to nothing voluntary on Hamlin's part, to nothing but the disappointing of her own perhaps unwarranted ideals; of making him understand that Hamlin's connection with Madame Elaguine, instead of being a grievance in her eyes, was the greatest happiness she could conceive. Perry was sure to burst out against Hamlin, to refuse to listen to her explanations, to insist upon fighting the battle of an injured woman.

Anne groaned at the thought, as she might have groaned at some immense stone to roll uphill. It was always so difficult for her to understand others, so intolerably more difficult to make herself understood. But she had resolved.

"I must tell you all my history since last we saw each other," she said; "you will want to hear it, won't you, Mr Perry?"

Perry, to whose brain all the unwonted splendour of this house, all the fantasticalness of finding his former nursemaid changed into a magnificently dressed goddess, had gone with a sort of narcotic effect, answered in a stupefied way, "Oh dear, yes—of course—I'm dying to hear it. I can't at all realise that it is really you, Annie, or really anybody and anything. Do you remember when we went into Lucca that day for the feast of the Holy Face, and I left you with Winnie and Mildred to go to the opera with Hamlin? D'you remember the plaster bust of Castruccio at the top of the hotel stairs, with the old woman's night-cap on? I don't know why that bust haunted me so. What tiny trots Winnie and Mildred were, with sashes down at their knees! and such confounded young flirts, five feet seven, as they are now! I see you have Winnie's photograph. How comic those brats must have looked! . . . But won't you tell me all your marvellous and incredible circumstances?"

"I scarcely know where to begin; perhaps I had better begin at the end. You wanted to know," said Anne, making a great effort to arrest Perry's attention, "why Mr Hamlin and I weren't married yet, nor even engaged . . ."

"Oh yes; what the deuce is the meaning of it, Annie? You are certainly the queerest people, you æsthetic folk. By Jove! you actually have a photograph of yourself with the children. I had clean forgotten its existence; and now I remember as if it were yesterday taking you to Alinari's, and how beastly naughty Winnie was! Oh, what a sulky blackamoor you do look, Annie! Good gracious! you don't mean to say you know *her*?" and Melton Perry suddenly turned the album, at which he was looking, towards Anne. "Where in the world did you pick up a photograph of Mrs Constantine Bulzo?"

"Mrs Constantine Bulzo?" asked Anne, in amazement. "Whom do you mean? I never heard of such a person. That photograph?—why, that's a half-Russian cousin of Mr Ham- lin's, Sacha Elaguine, who was a Miss Polozoff."

"Hamlin's cousin!" whistled Melton Perry,—"well, upon my word . . . yes, of course, I had forgotten—of course, her name isn't Mrs Constantine Bulzo any longer. But may I ask, how under heaven do you come to know Madame Elaguine?"

"I don't understand a word. This lady is Madame Elaguine; she is Mr Hamlin's first cousin, and that's of course how I come to know her."

"Hamlin's cousin or not Hamlin's cousin, how in the wide world could a woman like you ever know, ever meet such a—such a—excuse the word, but it's the least bad I can find—such an abominable baggage as this woman, Elaguine, or Bulzo, or Polozoff—as this abominable Sacha?"

Miss Brown turned white and almost green; the embroidery slipped out of her hands—she gasped.

"Good Lord, what's the matter with you, Annie?" cried Perry, jumping up; "you surely didn't imagine that—you surely can't be a great friend of such a creature as that. What's the matter?—are you ill?"

"It's nothing—the heat, I suppose," said Anne, stooping to pick up her embroidery; "and then, also, I suppose I'm not very strong yet; I've had brain fever, and you took me by surprise. But I oughtn't to have been surprised, because I know Sacha Elaguine has a great many enemies, and that her circumstances, her history, and in some measure, unfortunately, her ways and character, rather lend themselves to all manner of horrible stories. She's a frightfully tried and slandered little woman, poor thing. But I don't—I don't believe any of it."

Anne was conscious of a horrible effort as she spoke these words; lying was difficult to her; and she remembered Edmund Lewis's words.

"Are you really fond of Madame Bulzo—I mean Madame Elaguine?" asked Perry, grown very serious suddenly, and looking Anne in the face with an expression of surprise and pain. "Are you intimate with her?"

"I am intimate in the sense of having been with her a good deal, and knowing more than other people about her," answered Anne; "but I can't say I am a great friend of hers. She is Mr Hamlin's cousin; she has settled in England recently; he—we, I mean—see a good deal of her. I am awfully sorry for her, poor little woman; but there isn't very much in common between us."

"Thank goodness!" cried Perry. "Do you know, the sight of that photograph made me feel quite sick—the thought that you, Annie, should be the friend of such a creature. But I knew you couldn't be."

"But I am Madame Elaguine's friend; I don't believe a word of the infamous stories that are told about her; and you wouldn't believe them either, if you knew all that I do."

"What *do* you know ?" asked Perry, slowly and pityingly; "about the iniquities of Monsieur Elaguine, about the terrible persecution, the bits of letters, the pistol-shots, the poisoned chocolate, the lit spirits of wine poured under the door,—all that crazy imposture, I suppose? Well, I hope that Hamlin knows no more than you; otherwise, by God! he's no better than a blackguard to let you associate with this woman, be she his cousin a hundred times over; and you must never see that woman again, Annie. I forbid you to—I, as the oldest friend you have in the world—I forbid you to defile yourself by knowing that infamous creature." And Perry walked fiercely up and down, while Miss Brown, her whole body, it seemed to her, melting away from her soul, sat speechless looking at him.

"Listen to me, Anne," he said, "and judge whether I am unfair. God knows I'm not a Puritan, neither towards myself nor towards others. I've been a very rowdy man; I've knowu a great many rowdy women—what you call regular bad women—Russians, who are the worst of all—by the dozen. I'm not a red-tapist; I can quite understand women misbehaving,—having lovers—that sort of thing,—or even, if they are very wretched, selling themselves. It's beastly immoral to say so before a woman, but still, there it is, it's the truth. Well, such as you see me, I wouldn't touch *that* woman with the longest pair of tongs in all the devil's kitchen. That woman is really wicked—not merely immoral, but abominable, atrocious; she is the sort of woman who absolutely degrades a man, takes a pleasure in turning him into a beast and a madman—whose greatest pleasure would be to degrade and make a beast of an honest woman. Just listen to me. Some five years ago I knew a Greek couple—a young man and his sister, called Constantine and Marie Bulzo. They were orphans, very young, very handsome, especially the boy, who was only eighteen or nineteen. They were a sort of half-English Greeks, and went in for being æsthetical and artistic, all that sort of thing. I knew them in Florence, where Miss Bulzo, who was four or five years older than her brother, was studying painting. I gave them both lessons. I never met two such beautiful creatures, body and soul, as those young Bulzos. They were like young saints, and yet perfectly childish and merry, and they were quite devoted to each other: Marie really lived only for the boy. Well, six months later I met the two at Venice. They were staying at the same hotel as your Madame Elaguine, who immediately proceeded to make herself awfully fascinating and pathetic to them. Of course the poor children swallowed all about the persecutions by the Nihilists as so much

Gospel. They introduced me, and Madame Elaguine rather amused me; but I saw very soon that she wasn't a woman for them to know. There was a man staying in the same hotel, an old friend of hers, and, in fact, her lover, who was one of the vilest scoundrels the world ever bred—a horrible loathsome old Russian. I used to wonder how Madame Elaguine could endure him, but then I found out that he paid her bills for her. I tried to warn the Bulzos, especially Constantine, as, being a man, he might be expected to understand such things rather better. But, *figurati!* (and Perry made an expressive gesture of Italian exaggeration,) they wouldn't hear a word against their beloved, deeply injured, martyrised Madame Elaguine. Well, we half quarrelled; I scarcely saw anything of them. At the end of four months what do I hear, but that Miss Bulzo was married to Madame Elaguine's loathsome Russian; and then, a week later, I see Constantine and Madame Elaguine go off in the train together. Do you understand? Madame Elaguine, who was in love with young Bulzo, wanted to go off with him, and not knowing what to do with Marie, and wishing to dismiss and settle accounts with her *quondam* lover, had, in some fiendish way, induced this innocent girl of twenty-four to marry this frightful old Russian sinner—had sold her to the loathsome beast as a settlement to their debts; and Marie, after a few months, simply pined away and died of shame and disgust at the slavery she had been sold into. Do you understand that?"

"I understand; but I don't see why I should believe—it's too horrible to be true."

"It is true, though, for Constantine Bulzo told it me all himself later; how the Elaguine had talked him over to consent, and had regularly bullied his sister into the marriage, by pretending that it was the only way of paying a lot of imaginary debts of her brother's, and had forced Constantine, who was raving in love with her, to hold his tongue. That was the end of Marie Bulzo. Now as to Constantine. His sister once safely married to her old beast, he went off with the Elaguine, or rather, the Elaguine went off with him. Next summer I met them at Perugia; they were travelling about in remote places as Mr and Mrs Bulzo; and English people were so kind as to believe that this Russian woman of thirty and this Greek boy of twenty were married. Constantine perfectly adored her; but I never saw a man more changed: he looked thirty, a miserable, hang-dog, effeminate sort of creature, quite unable to do anything except drag after his so-called wife. That woman had regularly ruined the poor boy, broken his spirit, turned him into a kind of male odalisque of hers. Two years later the Bulzos were at Venice again; and I came just in time for the catastrophe. One fine morning Mrs Constantine Bulzo, become Madame Elaguine once more, packed her trunks and went off with a French painter, leaving her supposed husband to pay the hotel bill."

"I saw Constantine shortly after; the woman had spent nearly all his money, and he was living, or starving, in a room in a beastly court, slinking out only early in the morning and late at night, spending the day lying in his bed, eating opium and drinking. I never saw such a wreck in my life. As he was starving, I got him a place as clerk at a picture-shop, and tried to get him to work; but he didn't seem to care about living, and went on drinking and stupefying himself, till one day he drowned himself in the lagoon—they say accidentally, but I shall never believe it. That is the story of your Madame Elaguine; and I swear to you I have not exaggerated one word of it. Do you still think she is a woman fit to be known by you? By heaven! when I think what that miserable boy was when I saw him last, and what he had been when first I knew him, I feel as if it would be the greatest possible pleasure to throttle your Madame Elaguine with my own hands! Upon my soul, I do!"

Perry was walking up and down rapidly. Anne had never seen him so excited in his life.

"But," remarked Miss Brown, coldly, "even admitting your story to be true, which I suppose, as it comes from you, that I must, was it all the woman's fault? You men always throw the blame on the woman. But your Constantine Bulzo must have been a wretched weak creature."

Perry stopped short.

"No one has a right to expect every man or every woman to be very strong," he answered, sadly. "This poor boy was kind and trusting, and, when left to his own devices, honest. He was not weaker than most men, especially than most artistic natures—not weaker, for instance, than Walter Hamlin."

Anne Brown did not answer. But next morning she greatly surprised Melton Perry by asking him, in a voice that affected him as being very strange—

"Did you tell me something—a dreadful story—about Madame Elaguine and a young Greek friend of yours, yesterday afternoon?"

Perry looked at her with surprise. There was something in her wide-opened, strained eyes, in her rigidity of features, that made him think of a sleep-walker.

"Of course I did. Why?"

"Oh, nothing. I had only a very bad night—all manner of horrible dreams, and I was not sure whether this might not be one of them."

CHAPTER VIII.

"**DO** you know, Annie," said Melton Perry, two or three days later, "I find Watty very much altered. He seems so fearfully depressed and broken-spirited. He used always to be bored, but not like this; he has got to look so old, with those great rings under his eyes."

Miss Brown did not answer. Hamlin had returned the previous evening from Paris, and she also had noticed that he was changed—not so much, indeed, as Melton Perry seemed to think, for Melton Perry had not seen him for four or five years; and she—she had watched a change coming over him during the last months. Yet even she must own to herself that this change had made rapid progress during his fortnight or three weeks in Paris, or at least that this absence enabled her to notice the change much more. He was even more than usually apathetic and silent, and his pleasure at seeing his old friend once more was so slight, or rather so tempered by a kind of indifference and even annoyance, that Miss Brown felt perfectly nervous lest poor warm-hearted Melton Perry should feel mortally wounded. The next day Hamlin made an effort over himself: he seemed anxious to be as kind as possible to Perry; but somehow it did not succeed. Melton Perry would have liked, as he said, to have Walter all to himself, to sit with him by the hour together, or walk out alone with him, talking of old times; but Hamlin seemed possessed by a nervous dread of a *tête-à-tête*. He could not sit in the studio with Perry for more than half an hour without, on some excuse or other, calling his aunt or Miss Brown. He seemed to have invited a lot of people to drop in at all hours, as if to protect him from his old friend.

"It's awfully good of old Hamlin to wish me to know all these grand swell painters and newspaper writers," said Perry to Anne, in the tone of a disappointed child; "and I suppose it *is* very useful to me. But still, I wish I could get him to understand that what I want at present is to see just him and you; that all these confounded influential people will keep; and that I'd rather have a good talk over a pipe with him alone, as in old days."

Anne did not answer. It seemed to her that she understood so well why Hamlin dreaded a *tête-à-tête* with Melton Perry; a *tête-à-t;ête* which would be, largely, a talk about the past and the future, about her, Anne Brown. But Anne could not think about poor Perry and his disappointed friendliness; her whole nature seemed to be staggering and reeling, and the concerns of other folk were as distant, as unattainable, as they might be to a person tossed for hours on a stormy sea, paralysed, removed as it were from the world by an unspeakable sense of nausea. The days seemed to reel past, and yet not a week was gone since the arrival of Melton Perry.

One afternoon, they were seated—Hamlin, Perry, and she—with Mrs Macgregor at tea in the dim, shuttered drawing-room, with the heavy scent of flowers, when Richard Brown was announced. If a ghost had appeared on the threshold, Anne could not have turned paler, and trembled harder in all her limbs—this man, whom she had seen but a week ago, seemed indeed a spectre out of the past, the long dead past, with which all connection was severed. It was an immense relief to her not to be alone; she had an instinct that Richard had come to ask her whether, at last, she had settled matters with Hamlin; she thought she could see his eyes going from Hamlin's face to her own inquiringly. The conversation was languid and indifferent. Richard Brown wished for an explanation from her; Melton Perry hoped for an explanation from Richard Brown; Hamlin looked on passively, with that half-stupefied look which she had noticed in him lately.

Hamlin was more than merely depressed, he was very sad; his face, so handsome and still so young, so perfectly unmarked in feature, contrasted strikingly with the pleased, happy-go-lucky, kindly face of Perry; with the strong, eager, contemptuous face of Brown. For a moment Anne wondered what this sadness meant; whether there was in him any recollection of what he was, of what he might be; whether the poet, the dreamer, the chivalrous Hamlin of former days, still existed and suffered within this weak and degraded Hamlin of the present; and then, suddenly, this thought came in violent contact with the remembrance of Perry's story of Constantine Bulzo. Had Constantine Bulzo looked like that?

Richard Brown, obviously disappointed in his visit, rose.

"Why are you going so soon, Brown?" asked Hamlin, rising and making an effort over himself; "you never give me a chance of seeing you. Won't you stay to dinner? It is very impertinent of me to invite people in a house that isn't mine; but I feel sure Miss Brown is disappointed in not having had any talk with you. Chough is coming to see Perry this evening, so you and your cousin might have a chat after dinner."

He spoke simply, in his quiet, subdued, melancholy voice. Richard Brown looked at him rapidly from head to foot; what was the meaning of this? And Anne felt herself growing very red. Had Hamlin guessed what she scarcely herself knew?

"Thank you," answered Richard; "I am dining with some of my would-be constituents to-night. You know," he said to Anne, "I am going into Parliament, I believe. I will return soon; many thanks, Mr Hamlin."

"I have a good many things to tell you, Nan," he said, as Miss Brown accompanied him to the room-door. "I have heard of a scholarship which I am sure you could take if you would cram for six months; and I want to ask you a lot of things also. I will come back in two or three days. Good-bye."

He squeezed her hand; and Anne felt her heart thump at that hand-squeeze, so frank and affectionate.

"Good-bye, Cousin Dick," she said. Her voice and eyes and hand lingered in that farewell, in a way quite unusual to her reserved and decided nature. She was saying goodbye she knew not exactly to what, but she felt that the farewell was the last, and that it meant farewell to her happiness.

Chough came to dinner and stayed during the evening.

When he and Hamlin had taken their departure, Perry remained for a few moments standing by the open window, looking vacantly at the trees, the outlines of the craft moored opposite, the long trails of moonlight on the water. Then he came back into the room, and began fiddling with some roses in a glass.

"Beautiful roses," he said, in an awkward drawl; "we have none like them in Italy. Why don't Italians cultivate flowers? What do you call this? Is it a La France? I never knew a turnip from a jasmine."

"I think it is a La France; I don't know," answered Anne, taking a candlestick off the dining-room mantelpiece. "I think I must leave you now. You will find a box of cigarettes on the sideboard. Forgive me, I feel so tired and stupid."

"One moment!" cried Perry. "It's a very disagreeable thing I have to say, Annie; but I think I ought to say it. I guessed it the second time I saw him already; but now I am quite sure of it—Hamlin drinks."

Anne did not answer.

"I don't mean to say that he gets drunk. But he drinks—spirits; I've seen him to-night after dinner, and I'm sure he's going to take more at home. There's no mistaking the look. It isn't that he takes much, not more than I or most men might take; but it is that he oughtn't to take any. He used, you know, never even to take wine, except with gallons of water. He can't take anything of the sort. I remember already when we were at college together, Watty was a teetotaller. It appears some people are like that; I've heard doctors say that it's not unusual in families where there has been much drinking: it's a sort of diseased sensitiveness to alcohol—it becomes a kind of poison. You know that Hamlin's father drank, and one of his uncles died of drink, and his brother is either dead or dying, somewhere in a *maison de santé*, of a sort of mixed *delirium tremens* and craziness. It's a thing," went on Perry, keeping his eyes fixed on the pattern of the Persian rug under his feet, "which grieves and alarms me horribly; and in which I feel that you are probably the only person who could have any influence with him. It's useless my speaking. He must have got in among a bad lot. That little Chough seems harmless enough;but I hear that he was very close with a nasty fellow called Lewis—a spiritualist, opium-eater, haschisch-eater, and heaven knows what. Does he see much of him now?"

"He has quarrelled with Edmund Lewis, I fancy."

"Ah—so much the better. Then this would evidently be the moment to act. Of course I know it will be awfully difficult and horrible for you; because he'll feel so miserably ashamed before you, and, of course, you will feel it almost as badly as he. But still, you are the only person that can influence him. You see he loves you, worships you, all that sort of thing. And I am sure you will have the courage to get over your repugnance to a disagreeable half-hour, won't you, Annie, for your own sake as well as his?"

"I will do my best," said Miss Brown.

CHAPTER IX.

MISS BROWN went up to her room slowly, and slowly proceeded to undress.

"You look very tired, miss," said her maid; "haven't you perhaps been overtiring yourself so soon after your illness? and don't you think you had better let me brush your hair for you?"

Anne shook her head; she had never consented to let any one wait upon her except when ill, with that odd feeling that she, a servant, had no right to have a servant; and the maid whom Hamlin considered as a sort of necessary institution for a woman in Miss Brown's position, had been virtually put at the disposal of Mrs Macgregor, whose constant fidgeting over her clothes, and tea, and coffee, and food, according to hygienic theories of thirty years back, might have afforded occupation not to two but to twenty maids. Anne really did look very worn out; more so than she had seemed these several weeks, thought the maid.

"No, thank you, Laura," said Miss Brown. She really did not feel at all as if she could sleep; she felt the blood rushing through every artery of her body, and a hot faintness overtake her.

"It won't do to make myself ill again," she said to herself. The doctor had said that for the present she must try and get as much sleep as possible; and she was a practical, methodical person. She brushed her hair, still in short wavy masses since it was cut during the fever, carefully, slowly. It seemed to her as if, in the half light, it looked more grey than black. She pulled out a few white hairs: they come early in hair as dark and wiry as hers. She folded her clothes methodically, as she used to fold the clothes of the little Perrys, put out her light and lay down.

"It won't do to make myself ill again," she said; and, closing her eyes, determined to sleep.

She remained stretched out rigidly, like a dead woman, her head straight on her pillows, and trying to keep her mind as rigid as her body. But it was of no use. She could not sleep; her blood and her thoughts seemed to throb furiously within her.

Anne's mind had been made up, quietly, methodically, much in the same way as her hair had been brushed and her clothes folded, already a good hour ago, when talking to Melton Perry; she had seen the necessity of a decision coming, had waited for the moment when the decision should be made, ever since she had heard that story of Madame Elaguine and Constantine Bulzo. There had been, it seemed to her, no alternative; and there seemed to her that there was no alternative now, either. But as she lay motionless in her bed, and stared into the darkness with wide-opened eyes, she began, once more, to go over slowly and repeatedly the steps of the argument, which had, three or four days ago, become manifest to her as might the mechanism of a broken watch to a watchmaker, of any very inevitable and obvious thing.

Hamlin had done everything for her; he had turned what she looked back upon with horror, as a kind of intellectual and moral death, into life. He had bought her soul free, had nourished and nurtured it, as a man might have redeemed, nourished, and nurtured the body of some slave child, doomed to be a cripple in a crippling occupation; he had done, she felt assured, what no other man had ever done for a woman, since no other woman, she thought, could have escaped from such a state of utter soul stagnation as had already begun, those five years ago, in her slow, sullen nature. It was more than had ever been done for another woman, and Anne felt its value more than any other; for despite the modesty and frankness which often took others aback, the very stuff of her soul, like the very mould of her features, was pride. She knew herself to be nobler than the majority of men and women; not more intelligent, nor more honest, nor more kindly, nor any one particular quality, but more homogeneous of nature; not alloyed in any portion, whatever she might be; upright, sincere, practical, harsh even, through and through: a reality, where they seemed but half reality and half make-up. And that she should be this she owed to Hamlin; without him she would have been equally homogeneous of soul, but it would have been with the uniformity, the rigidity of spiritual death.

What Hamlin had done, he had done from no base motives, and without the smallest taint of baseness in the doing: he had not actually wanted her, he had wanted merely to perfect a thing that seemed to him good of its sort, to make her a soul that should suit her body; he had done it deliberately, consistently, unwearyingly, with a gentleness, a generous tact, which had themselves been a benefit.

That Hamlin had acted from an imaginative whim, that he had carried out an exotic artistic caprice, played a sublimated game of artistic skill, Anne could not at this moment take into account. She knew, and only too well, that Hamlin was selfish, whimsical, fantastic, vain, a seeker after new *poses* and new sensations; but she knew all this analytically, piecemeal as the result of thought; and she was in a sense too dull, too unable to comprehend others, and, above all, too utterly devoid of all vanity, whimsicalness, and theatricality, too completely of a piece, a mass of granite, as she often felt, to conceive these analytically recognised peculiarities as absolutely organic and active forces. She had conceived Hamlin to be that which to her was the easiest conception—generous; and nothing could make her conceive his behaviour towards her in any any other light. Moreover, there remained in this frank and fearless nature, shrinking from no disillusions, one delusion which was the safer for her very consciousness of uncompromising hatred of all delusions. She clung, without knowing it, to the belief that in one thing at least Hamlin had been perfectly noble, that no subsequently discovered weakness and baseness could ever alter that; she treasured up a shred of her old ideal, the belief that whatever Hamlin might be towards others and towards himself, towards her he had been the real Hamlin whom she had loved and worshipped.

And now this Hamlin, this man to whom she owed all, and whose past she still loved, was gradually being alienated from all the nobler things for which he was fit—gradually being separated from his nobler self, and dragged, stripped of all his better qualities, into a moral quagmire, a charnel, a cloaca, to stick and rot inchwise. And this, Anne said to herself, to some degree by her own fault; for had she not let her antipathy for the tendencies which she had gradually discovered in him, and her loathing for the tendencies of the men who surrounded him, smother her gratitude, her sympathy, turn her away in sullen scorn and isolation, from the man whom she was bound to help, and the men whom she was bound to combat? She forgot for the moment the many abortive attempts she had made to awaken the better qualities of Hamlin; or rather, she could no longer conceive that those attempts had been sufficiently strenuous and determined; it seemed to her, forgetful of the dead-weight of opposition, that she must have been very feeble and half-hearted. Instead of thinking of him, she had thought only of herself, of preserving her own soul from infection, of keeping her own soul strong and active; she had selfishly thought of the world's miseries, which she could not prevent, instead of thinking of Hamlin, whom she might have saved; and finally, she had let herself indulge in dreams of liberty, that is to say, of deser- tion of her duty. Those monks and nuns of former days, for whom she felt such unutterable contempt, had they acted differently from her when they left their fellow-men to perish in sin, in order that they might enjoy the luxury of virtue in a convent or a desert? She loathed æsthetes like Hamlin; and yet, what had she herself been, save an æsthete of another sort, selfishly preoccupied with spiritual comfort, and worse than any of them for the very moral consciousness which lay at the root of this immorality?

Why had she not driven away Edmund Lewis, opposing herself to him with all her might? Why had she not driven away Sacha Elaguine? Now that she had learned from Melton Perry what this woman really was, every single circumstance of their former intercourse, every single fact and suggestion that had come to her, from Mrs Macgregor's warnings to Edmund Lewis's cowardly accusation,—all the hundred little impressions which she herself had received, grouped themselves together, and made it obvious that Sacha must be, could only have been, the horrible walking depravity which she had been revealed. Essentially unanalytic of mind, Miss Brown could now no longer conceive how it was that she had not understood Madame Elaguine at once; in that massive horror with which the Russian woman had filled her, it was impossible to remember all the deluding little circumstances which had closed her heart to suspicion—nay, all the purity of her own nature, the charity, the desire to be equitable, which had made this now so overpowering mass of abomination not merely impossible to realise, but impossible to conceive. It seemed to her as if Sacha must always have shown herself what she was; and that she, Anne Brown, must have wilfully closed her eyes. She had never asked herself whether it was not her duty towards Hamlin to come to some conclusion about his cousin; she had let their connection drift on; she had seen in the ruin of the man to whom she owed all, only a means to her own deliverance from a life which she hated, from a duty which she shirked. Anne remembered how she had watched with terror that look of weariness and shame on Hamlin's face, which ought to have told her that this poor, weak, sick soul might still be saved; she remembered the joy with which she had heard of Hamlin's departure for Paris—that is to say, of the crowning act of weakness and folly which had made him the chattel of his cousin. Anne loathed herself as a woman might loathe herself, who recognised that she had let some living creature die of hunger and want of nursing. Shame she did not feel, nor yet remorse; she cared too little for herself to care for her own ideals; she did not once think that she had been mistaken, that she had been base, ungrateful, that she was dishonoured in her own eyes; she merely thought that Hamlin was on the brink of ruin, ruin of all his nobler self and of his happiness—that she had done it, and that she was there, alone, to save him. In those long hours, lying motionless in the dark, the face of Hamlin, as she had recently seen it, that weak, profoundly depressed, half-degraded face, was constantly before her eyes; and surrounding it, vague and threatening, the faces—so strangely like it and transfigured in a kind of tragic degradation, of the portraits at Wotton Hall—of Hamlin's half-crazy, disgraced brother; of his odious, passion-stained father; of his drunken uncles; above all, that beautiful woman's face, with the curled hair and loose collar—that face so curiously compounded of effeminacy, whimsicalness, and cynical self-abandonment; of his great-uncle Mordaunt, whose portrait had been exiled to the lumber-room, whose name banished from the memory of his relatives; and along with them, and resembling them like a brother, the confused, imaginary image of that miserable Greek lad whom Sacha Elaguine had ruined.

Was it still time? Could Hamlin still be saved? was he already hopelessly bound for life to Madame Elaguine? Had Anne waked up too late? She did not know. She only knew that there was not an hour, not a moment to lose; and that there was but one thing to be done. Hamlin must not, should not, marry Sacha. And the only way to prevent it was that he should marry Anne Brown. He might, as Lewis said, and as she believed, already be the lover of Madame Elaguine; but he was not yet the husband, and most probably not yet the betrothed. And was he not bound, by that paper which the ignoble suspiciousness of Richard Brown had required of him in that distant past in Florence, to marry Anne Brown at whatever time she rnight call upon him to do so?

"I must become his wife," said Anne to herself; and she said it as she might have said "the sun must rise in so many hours." There was no room for hesitation on her part; the choice, the act of volition, was so decided, that there ceased to be either choice or volition; to become Hamlin's wife seemed to Anne as an inevitable necessity coming from without. But little by little: as she lay there broad awake, yet with somewhat of that tendency, as of an opium-dreamer, to see things exaggerated which comes to us in darkness, she began to realise the meaning of this formula—to become Hamlin's wife. The whole past rushed into her mind, and became, as it were, the mirage of the future, and that mirage was horrible. To be Hamlin's wife meant to relinquish the liberty which had, for the last two or three months, been safe within her grasp, the liberty of being herself. Anne was one of those natures which, though able, by moments, to enjoy themselves like children, do not believe much in happiness; to whom, singled out, as it were, to achieve self-sacrifice or endure martyrdom, happiness is a mere name, a negative thing—but to whom unhappiness is a positive reality, the thing which they expect, with which their soul seems, in some pre-natal condition, to have become familiar as the one great certainty. The happiness, therefore, which she was losing—the independence, the activity, the serenity, the possibility of a life of noble companionship with Richard Brown—all this was only a distant and unsubstantial thing; she had never experienced it, and it could not well be realised. But she knew by experience, familiar with its every detail, the unhappiness which lay in the future as Hamlin's wife, for this future would be but a return to the past; and she felt as might a person lost in a catacomb, and who, having got to a chink, having seen the light and breathed the air, should be condemned to wander again, to rethread for ever the black and choking corridors leading nowhere. That Hamlin was lost if he married Sacha, she knew as she knew that two and two make four; but she did not in the least flatter herself that her own influence would be as potent for good, as Madame Elaguine's must be potent for evil. She knew Hamlin too well for that, and herself also. If Hamlin had remained weak, cold, vain, and mean under her influence hitherto, he must remain so for ever; he was born all these things. She could prevent his growing worse, she could not make him grow better; her position would be as that of a woman who devoted herself to nurse a person sick of an incurable disease: there would be none of the excitement of a possible cure, only the routine, the anxiety peculiar to a case where the patient is for ever on the brink of getting worse.

To be understood, to be sympathised with, to be loved really and really to love—none of these things would be for her. But, after all, what right had she to any of them? Anne was, in all matters concerning herself, a born fatalist and pessimist; the words of Goethe, "Entbehren sollst du, sollst entbehren," were to her not an admonition, but a mere statement of fact. She had, for a time, fancied that she clutched happiness; if it had turned out, like the goddess clutched by Ixion, a mere mist, why, that was quite natural; there was nothing to complain of in that.

But suddenly there came a sense not any longer of the loss of happiness, but of a sickened revolt from all the things which this sacrifice of happiness implied. Not to love, not to be loved. Well, that was natural; but to submit to becoming the property of a man whom she did not love, and who could not, in her eyes, ever love her, that was another thing. Edmund Lewis and Madame Elaguine, learned in such matters, had been perfectly correct when they declared that Anne was, in their sense of the word, passionless, cold. To this woman, consumed by intellectual and moral passion, her womanhood meant merely the instincts of superior chastity, of superior soul cleanness, which seem the birthright of women, as the instincts of superior generosity, of superior soul energy, seem the birthright of men; and this, to her the only result of womanhood, merely added a positive element of repulsion to the disdain for what the world is pleased to call love already existing in her. Anne Brown, born of the people, grown up as a servant, left to take care of herself when scarcely more than a child, and then thrust into the midst of a demoralised school of literature which gloried in moral indifference,—Anne Brown had none of those misty notions of marriage so easily transfigured into poetry, and which make (and perhaps fortunately) many clean-souled and disdainful girls enter unconsciously and unabashed upon a life frequently neither very noble nor very clean. Without formulating it to herself—for she never formulated anything—Miss Brown had a very strong sense that marriage without love was a mere legalised form of prostitution. To become, therefore, the wife of Hamlin, was an intolerable self-degradation—nay, a pollution; for it seemed to her, and the idea sickened her whole soul, that the moral pollution of Sacha Elaguine would be communicated to her. To become the wife of Sacha's lover! Her limbs seemed to give way, to dissolve; a horrible warm clamminess overtook her; she could not breathe, or breathed only horror.

Anne rose from her bed, and wrapping her-self in her dressing-gown, sat down by the window, partly ajar. She threw it wide open, pulled up the blinds, and, gasping, looked out into the darkness. The sky was covered, not a ray of light; it was raining—she heard the drops fall heavily on the leaves under the window; a warm damp gust of air blew in her face. Anne did not know what it was to faint, and her limbs did not give way beneath her; but she felt as if her mind, her soul, were fainting, growing clammy—slipping, slipping away, dissolving into nothingness. To be the wife of Sacha's lover! With the scornful aversion which a woman of actively chaste nature (for the virtue exists in most women only in a negative, passive condition) experiences for the more abstract idea of weakness and unchastity, was mingled—perhaps not very clearly to herself—somewhat already of the wrath of the outraged wife. Under her very eyes, before all the world, Hamlin had deceived her—had been another woman's lover—and had let her associate with his mistress! the kind of resentment which the world sometimes mistakes for jealousy, but into which there enters no love,—the sense not of being neglected as an individual, but being insulted as a woman. To be the wife of Sacha's lover! Anne's imagination—slow in all things, and slowest where any ignoble or impure thing was concerned—was trailed as by an inexplicable force along a dim tract of foulness.

No; she could not marry this man. She had no right to forego her just resentment, to stifle her just disgust, no right to degrade her soul in order to save his. If he was weak, vain, foredoomed to baseness, let him run his career—fulfil his destiny. Some sacrifices are sins. Without identifying the case, Anne's thoughts reverted to the story, to the words of Isabella in 'Measure for Measure'; and the pride that lay at the bottom of her soul—the pride of purity and strength—rose like a great wind within her. No; she would not pollute her cleanness, prostitute her nobility, for this man. Anne folded her dressing-gown close about her, and extended her strong fingers tight over the arms of her chair—a movement like that of a judge about to pronounce a sentence. Any one who could have seen her sitting thus by the window—who could have seen that pale stern face, those wide-opened onyx-grey eyes looking steadfastly into the darkness—would have said that this magnificent young woman with the tragic features was capable of cold cruelty.

But though in some measure right, since there is a destructive element in all strong souls, the person who should have thought like this would yet have been mistaken. Anne's ruthlessness, her cruelty, could exist only against herself; the sacrifice, which seemed to her no very great matter, was the sacrifice of herself.

Anne remained seated for a few minutes by the window, that storm of pride and contempt rushing in great gusts through her whole nature. But then suddenly the storm dropped.

Here was Hamlin, to whom she owed everything, owed this very soul which seemed too good to be wasted upon him, in danger of being degraded for ever by this loathsome woman, this incarnation of all his own vices, this moral disease become a human creature. This fate **must** be averted, Hamlin **must** be saved, for his own sake and for the sake of the world—of all those nobler things that he might still do; he must be saved, and only one thing could save him—hence that one thing must be done. Anne rose from the window. This darkness unnerved her. She struck a light and lit the candles on the mantelpiece; they were in clustered candlesticks, and the room was brilliantly illuminated. Anne looked round her. There was a heap of books and papers on her table,—she had been interrupted in tidying them the previous day. She began to put them to rights. Some of the books were the manuals of political economy and works on philosophy which she was studying with a view to Girton. The sight of them made a knot rise in her throat and the tears come into her eyes. She felt that she would never read them again. She took them in her arms, and opening the lowest drawer of her writing-table, locked them up. "I will give them to Marjory's women's club," she thought. Then she opened another drawer, and got out all her note-books and copy-books,—her many months' work, ever since Richard Brown had first lent her his primer. She turned over a few pages slowly. The sentences seemed to have no meaning; her brain refused to act. She took the papers one by one and tore them into small shreds, and threw them into the waste-paper basket. "There is an end of that," she said to herself quietly. Anne looked round the room once more,—at the spruce Queen Anne furniture which had surprised her so much, at the blue and white vases, the shimmering plates, the pieces of embroidery on the wall—all the things which Hamlin had put there to please her. Was there anything more—anything more to be done? On the mantelpiece stood a photograph of Richard Brown, unframed, which he had recently given her: she had asked him for a photograph during Hamlin's absence with Sacha. She took the photograph and held it over one of the candles; it curled up, charred, only the rim which she held remaining to show what it had been; she turned it round and round over the flame, and then threw the crumpled piece of charred pasteboard into the grate.

The first pale light of dawn was beginning to mingle with the light of the candles, making them burn yellow, and surrounded by a sort of halo, like the tapers round a catafalque. Outside she saw the chilly grey streaks of light, the faint cold rose veinings of sunrise. But the sunrise itself did not come; the sky gradually appeared, clotted with red and purplish reflections; then the colour died away, and there remained instead a pale, suffused, grey heaven. It began to drizzle. Anne left the window. The room was light now with daylight—the candle-flames mere yellow specks. Anne put them out; she pulled down the blinds and got into bed, and again stretched herself out in that stiff way, her head propped up on the pillows, trying not to think. In a few minutes she was asleep.

When the maid came in, she did not wake up as usual, and the girl was half-frightened and very much awed by seeing Miss Brown lying straight and motionless; her face, surrounded by a sort of wreath of short, curling, iron-black locks, stiff on the pillow, looking, in the grey morning light which came through the pale-blue blinds, like a dead woman.

Anne opened her eyes and looked round slowly, as if trying to collect her thoughts. "Ah," she said, half audibly, "I remember."

CHAPTER X.

BY an effort of manoeuvring which was not very natural to her, Miss Brown induced Melton Perry to take himself off after breakfast and go and see some studios, an expedition which would keep him out of the way till lunch. She would have Hamlin all to herself. When Perry was gone, Anne sat down to write to Mary Leigh, who was in the country. There was absolutely no reason why she should write to Mary, nor had she anything whatever to tell her; but she was devoured by a restlessness—by a vague desire to talk to some one who cared for her. She told Mary Leigh nothing of what was passing through her mind, nor of the event which was pending: there was not, in her letter, a word to suggest anything of the sort; but there was in it the expression, vague and without motives, of the great emotion which occupied her soul. "I want to tell you, dear Mary," wrote Anne, "how grateful I am for the affection which you and Marjory have shown towards me lately. If I had died of that illness, it would have been a great consolation to know that you cared for me so much." She did not know why, the tone of the whole letter, with all these expressions of gratitude, had the solemnity of a farewell, as if written by a woman who expected to die soon. And Anne really felt as if her life were coming to an end.

When she had finished writing, she went down to Hamlin's studio. He would come soon, and she would wait for him here.

It was still drizzling, and the room opening on to the garden, with its silk blinds drawn down, was full of a kind of twilight. Anne walked up and down for a minute or two, looking vaguely round her. A drowsy scent of faded flowers, of cigarette-smoke, of she knew not what scent, made her feel weak and dreamy, and reminded her, with a movement of disgust, of Sacha Elaguine's rooms. She had not been in the studio of late, except for a few minutes at a time. Everything seemed to her untidy and dusty—easels and boards thrown about in a way which was not usual with Hamlin. She looked vaguely at the various things,—at the drawings by Rossetti and Burne Jones on the walls, the books in cases, the terra cottas and bits of carving on brackets, the piano with the brocade cover thrown back, and the score of Wagner's Tristram still on the desk. She looked at the score and played a few notes, but stopped. She loathed that music which Hamlin and Sacha so admired—that music, with its strange, insidious faintings and sobbings, its hot, enervating gusts of passion. On the mantelpiece, among the Japanese jars, the bronze lamps, and other similar properties, her eye caught a small bottle of blue glass. She took it up: it was not labelled, or the label was removed, but it left a sort of sickly-smelling stickiness on her fingers. So Perry was right; Hamlin had returned to his old practice of taking opium. She put the bottle back, and walked up and down once more. Then her eye fell upon an unfinished portrait of herself, or what was intended to be herself, which stood in the shadow. A solemn sombre woman in green, with very blue peaks and glaciers in the distance, twisting the faded green leaves of a palm-branch. It was the picture which Hamlin had begun long, long ago in Florence; and her mind went back to that other rainy day, as gloomy as this one, seemingly centuries ago, when she had stood in the tower studio, about to take leave of Hamlin, as she thought, for the last time. Was she really as sombre as that picture? thought Anne. On a table, gritty with dust, lay an open sketch-book; Anne took it up listlessly. The sheet was scrawled with several versions of an allegorical design, feebly drawn, scarcely more than outlined, and, as it seemed, in a moment of weariness. A beautiful naked youth was clutched by a huge, haggard woman, her torn dress licking his body like flames, her lips greedily advancing to his delicate face, which shrank back, like a flower withering in the heat of a furnace. There were several versions, crossing and recrossing each other oddly, but always the same flower-like winged boy writhing in the terrible breath of this embrace, always that fainting beautiful face, and those burning lips with the suction of flame. Beneath one of the versions was scrawled, "Amor a Libidine interfectus," and a few lines, half scratched out, of a sonnet. Anne did not read them; she put down the sketch-book. She knew the sense of that allegory, even before her eye caught the words, "and thus my soul," which formed one of the lines of the rough-scrawled sonnet. Anne shuddered. Steps came along the corridor—Hamlin's steps. She sat down near the window, for she expected her heart would have begun beating even to bursting. But it was not so; Miss Brown felt wonderfully calm.

"I want to talk to you about something, Mr Hamlin," she said, when he had recovered from the surprise of finding her in the studio. "You have nothing very pressing to do just now, I hope?"

"Nothing," answered Hamlin; "I am at your disposal." He sat down opposite to her, and began to fidget with the pencils and pen-knives lying on the table. He was very pale, haggard, and looked tired and worried.

"You don't seem well," said Anne, mechanically.

"I am horribly nervous, that's all," he answered, passing his hand through his hair. "I suppose it's this damp heat. Will it annoy you if I smoke a cigarette? I feel my brain spinning."

Anne nodded, and waited in silence till he had taken two or three puffs.

"Mr Hamlin," she suddenly began, in a low, steady voice, rather like a person reciting a lesson, "it is going on three years since I left Coblenz and came into this house. I am over twenty-four, and I don't think it is possible to continue much longer on the theory that I am your ward. It is time that something should be decided about my future."

Hamlin listened quietly, with a certain listless and helpless look that was very painful.

"I quite agree with you," he answered, "and I fully see how greatly I am to blame in not having forestalled you. You must not suppose that I have not thought more than once about this matter. I have done so, I assure you. But somehow, things have always come in the way; and then, you know, I—I did not wish to put any pressure upon you. In short, I am unable to say how it is that I have placed myself in what may appear to be the wrong in this matter."

Again he passed his hand across his head.

"Forgive me," he said, "for being so feeble this morning. I really have a wretched headache."

Miss Brown, Vol. 3

"I am very sorry for you," answered Anne, but adding with the same deliberate resolution, "but all the same, I feel that I can no longer delay, and that I must avail myself of this opportunity to ask you a question. Have you any intention of marrying me?"

Hamlin, who had been sitting with his head resting on his hand, vacantly watching the wreathing smoke of his cigarette, suddenly looked up at Anne. She was seated very erect in a high-backed chair opposite, looking taller, calmer than ever, less girlish than ever also, although he had never thought of her, even years ago, as a girl. He looked at her for a moment in silence; a long, lingering, and very melancholy look.

"Miss Brown," he answered, and his voice became tremulous towards the end of his speech, "you have, if you remember the terms of our reciprocal engagement, always been free; and you are free. It is rather sad for me to reflect—and perhaps a little sad for you also—how very differently things have turned out from what I believe both of us anticipated. And it is, as you may understand, not a little sad to part with what has been the best thing in my life—to end my best episode. But you must remember that I never wished you to be otherwise than perfectly independent; it has been a great matter in a useless life like mine to have contributed to reinstate you, as it were, in your birthright; it will be something to think of later, that I have been conducive in making you what you are; and"—Hamlin had risen from his chair and stretched out his hand—"will you believe me also when I say that I am very, very happy that you have found a man whom you can love and respect, and who can make you happy?"

Hamlin's mouth, that delicate mouth with the uncertain lines, began to quiver. Anne turned very red, and then, suddenly, very white. She did not take his hand; she did not look at him as he stood before her; her eyes seemed fixed in space, as she answered in a voice which became steadier and louder as she went on—

"You don't understand me. I was not alluding to any notion of marrying my cousin. I don't want to marry Richard. What I want to ask you is this: Will you marry me, Mr Hamlin?"

Anne, spoke very slowly, gravely, and calmly; but as she spoke, she felt her heart tighten. There remained still one chance, one shred of hope, and in another moment that might be gone.

A sudden convulsion passed over Hamlin's face; he caught at the back of a chair, for he seemed trembling and reeling, his eyes closed for a moment as if he were choking, and he made a vague helpless movement with one hand, as a man who cannot speak. Then, suddenly, he flung himself down before Miss Brown's chair, seized both her hands, and covered his face with them.

"Anne—Anne!" he cried.

They remained thus for a moment; she seated upright in the chair, he on his knees, her hands pressed to his face.

"Anne—you love me," he murmured.

Miss Brown did not answer. She looked straight before her into space, fixedly, vaguely, taking in nothing, with her solemn, tearless, grey eyes. She felt as if she were waiting she knew not for what, counting the tickings of an unheard clock.

"You love me, Anne; you love me!" cried Hamlin, louder; and pressing closer to her, he put out his arms, and drew down her face to his, and kissed her, twice, thrice, a long kiss on the mouth.

It seemed to Anne as if she felt again the throttling arms of Sacha Elaguine about her neck, her convulsive kiss on her face, the cloud of her drowsily scented hair stifling her. She drew back, and loosened his grasp with her strong hands.

Hamlin sprang up. His face was changed: he was radiant. He took her hand in both his, and looked long into her eyes.

"Forgive me," he whispered; "forgive me—oh, forgive me, Anne. That all this time I should have been so blind—thought you indifferent and contemptuous. Oh, forgive me for all my wickedness, my folly; forgive me, my darling, for not having understood that I belonged to you, that you loved me."

Anne nodded without speaking. She could not tell a lie, even now; and she knew she must not tell the truth. Yet never perhaps had she loathed Hamlin as she loathed him—vain, fatuously happy—at this moment that he believed she had confessed that she loved him.

"Well, then," she said quickly, "perhaps you can understand that—after what has passed, you understand—I am anxious that we should get married at once. Perry was asking me, only the other day, why things had dragged on so long; and then also there is . . ."

"I understand," interrupted Hamlin. "Oh, forgive me, dearest. I never, never really loved that woman: I could not have loved her. I have never loved but you. Will you believe it?"

"You will never see her again?—I mean, never except in my presence? " went on Anne. "Will you promise that? And will you promise to leave London in a day or two—to go to Italy, anywhere where she is not—and wait till I can join you with Aunt Claudia?"

"I promise; I will do anything. Oh, Anne, if only you will forget all that; if you will believe me when I tell you that I never loved that woman—that I felt the whole time that she was debasing, humiliating me, making me forfeit all my honour and my happiness . . ."

Anne paid no attention to these assurances. So he was shifting all the shame of his weakness and baseness and sensuality on to another,—washing his hands of the woman who had given herself to him. How like him! How well, how terribly well, Anne knew him!

"You have promised, remember," she repeated,—"you will leave to-morrow, the day after—as soon as you can. You won't tell her where you are going—do you understand? You will write to-day, and tell her of our marriage, and that you have promised never to see her again."

Hamlin kissed her hand with passion.

"And listen," went on Miss Brown; "this evening there is a big party at the Argiropoulos. I did not intend going; but I wish to go now. Write to Mrs Argiropoulo to tell her we are coming together; explain that we are going to be married; ask her to tell all her guests. I want every one to know. Do you understand, Mr Hamlin—Walter, I mean? You won't lose time, will you?"

"No, no!" cried Hamlin; "I understand. Only forgive me; and tell me that you love me, my darling;" and he seized Anne, and kissed her again with a sort of fury. "Tell me that you forgive me for all that I have made you suffer, Anne. Speak,—only one word, Anne—one word."

Anne covered her eyes with her hand.

"I forgive you, Walter," she answered, and burst into tears. But she wiped them away, and, rising suddenly, left the room.

"Walter is leaving for Italy to-morrow," she said, as she met Melton Perry in the corridor. "I want you to accompany me and Aunt Claudia there in a few days. Mr Hamlin and I are going to be married."

"God bless my soul!" cried Perry. "When—where—why didn't you tell me before?" But Anne was out of sight.

CHAPTER XI.

IN the blazing drawing-room, where a crowd of black coats and shining bare shoulders and fashionable dresses contrasted drolly with the melancholy thin Cupids of Burne Jones, the mournful mysterious ladies of Rossetti, which adorned the walls, one of Mrs Argiropoulo's many musical celebrities was wailing Austrian popular songs at the piano. Miss Brown, who had undergone the universal staring and received the general congratulations with a monosyllabic composure much criticised on all hands, had slipped away, when the Austrian tenor approached the piano, to the furthest end of the room, where she was half protected from sight by the plants of an adjacent conservatory. All this triumph, people said to them- selves, as they looked round at her seated alone in the corner, dressed in a wonderful garment of cloth-of-silver, resting her dark head on her hand, was too much even for her. Yet in reality Miss Brown did not feel any emotion; she was too tired for that. She felt as if she had just finished a long journey, or as she used sometimes to do years ago after a hard morning's ironing in summer—weary, broken, too numb for thought or for pain. The guttural voice of the Austrian tenor, wailing out the simple little mountain songs, which would at any other time have brought the tears into her eyes and a thought of death into her heart, seemed to her vague and distant like a voice in a dream; and like a crowd seen through a mist seemed all these very concrete men and women all about her. As the last notes of the song died away, she felt the touch of a fan, the downy stroke of a bunch of feathers, on her neck. It was Madame Elaguine behind her; but the sight of Madame Elaguine caused Anne no emotion, and she followed the Russian woman, who beckoned her into the neighbouring conservatory, in the same absent way as she had answered the congratulations of her acquaintances.

"You are very tired, Annie dear," said Madame Elaguine, in one of her caressing half–whispers, but fixing her eyes on Miss Brown with a look which was anything but a caress. "All this emotion—this general ovation and triumph, this great joy of satisfied love—has been too much for you, poor child!"

Anne shook her head, thrown back on the Persian embroidery of an ottoman, among the large tropical leaves and the delicate stems of bamboos and fern plants. She knew that this woman wished to insult her; but she was too weary and absent–minded to care.

"I am merely rather tired. I didn't get much sleep last night," she answered, as she might have answered the maid who pulled up her blinds in the morning. Madame Elaguine seemed a hundred miles away from her: she shrank neither from a woman whom she loathed, nor from a woman who, she felt, was bent upon insulting her.

She did not feel Madame Elaguine's glance, although the glance was concentrated hatred and outrage.

"Poor child!" repeated Sacha, taking one of her hands and pressing it between her own burning ones. "Poor child! Ah, well, I won't bore you with congratulations. I know Walter sufficiently well to know how happy he will make you; and I know how deeply you have loved him all the while, and how faithfully he has always loved you. But I want to give you a little wedding–present. I have brought it here, because Walter has written to me that you don't want to have your bliss disturbed, and are going off at once. Quite right. When people are very happy, there's something immodest in letting the world see it and be jealous; that's the classic view, isn't it?" As she spoke she drew from out of her cloud of lace and feather trimmings a little leathern case.

"Oh dear no," went on Madame Elaguine, "you mustn't think I've been ruining myself. I'm far too much of a pauper and far too selfish to go making handsome presents. It doesn't cost me anything, you see, for Walter gave me them last month; and as I really don't care a jackstraw about pearls, and I accepted them merely to please him, I think it's much better you should have them to make the set complete, since you have the necklace."

The case contained two large pearl ear-rings, which Anne immediately recognised as part of the set once belonging to Hamlin's mother which he had shown her long ago at Wotton. Round her own neck was the former Mrs Hamlin's pearl necklace; he had given it to her that evening, not a fortnight, perhaps, since giving Sacha the ear-rings.

Anne looked at the ear-rings for a moment, feeling the triumphant eyes of Sacha upon her; she felt also her face grow crimson, and her soul waking out of its state of lethargic indifference, with a fierce desire to tear the pearls off her own throat, and crush them into the carpet with her foot.

"Thank you," she merely said, closing the box and handing it back to Sacha; "I don't think I could wear them, Madame Elaguine. And I don't think my husband would wish me to wear them," she added, but the words half stuck in her throat.

"Won't you, really?" said the Russian. "I assure you Walter will be most mortified if he hear that you have refused them. It would be a hundred pities that the set should be spoilt. I wouldn't have taken these, if he hadn't told me that I should have the rest. You see, I was the nearest of kin last month. And I'm sure it would make poor Aunt Philippa turn in her grave to know that all her things did not go to Miss Anne Brown. Ah, well—as you like. I can always get them exchanged at the jeweller's for something else—or I'll tell Walter, and he can buy them back for you. That's more like a pauper's proceeding."

"Thank you, Madame Elaguine," said Anne, preparing to rise, "I think I ought to go and talk to some of the people in the next room."

But Madame Elaguine laid hold of her wrist. "Don't go yet, my dear Madonna of the Glaciers—I shan't see you again, perhaps, for a long while, and I want you to tell me some things. I'm a horrible ill-bred little creature, I know, but I can't help it. I've always had a lot of morbid curiosities. One of them is how love-marriages are made up—how it all comes about. You see I wasn't married for love—I was married for money by my Russian relations. But I always think I should like to know about love-marriages. Tell me what Walter said to you—how he did it. I wish I'd seen it."

Anne's face was burning. Each of Madame Elaguine's words was a piece of insolence.

"Did you always love him—ever since the beginning—ever since he sent you to school; and have you always gone on caring for him in the same way?" went on Madame Elaguine. "Fancy, I thought you didn't care much for Walter, almost disliked him; I almost thought you were in love with your big black cousin. It was like my obtuseness! Do tell me all about it . . ."

"There is nothing to tell you, Madame Elaguine," said Anne. "Mr Hamlin and I are going to be married, that's all."

"In short," answered Madame Elaguine, bursting into an angry laugh, "you thought better of it; you learned to appreciate the satisfaction of getting a handsome husband, with a good name and a good fortune. I think you are quite right. Mrs Hamlin of Wotton sounds better than Mrs Richard Brown. Or else are you still sufficiently human to enjoy making a man give the cold shoulder to another woman? I fear I must spoil your satisfaction in this. I have never cared a button for Walter. I would not have married Walter for anything you could offer me; I only cared to bring down his pride a little, in remembrance of the days when his great virtue of seventeen had me turned out of my uncle's house, like a housemaid who has made love with the butler. As to Walter himself, you are welcome to him, though I don't promise that some day the whim may not return to me to amuse myself a little more at his expense." Miss Brown looked at Madame Elaguine with disgust: this delicate charming little creature seemed suddenly transformed into Mrs Perry's housemaid Beppa, whom she had overtaken one day, years ago in Florence, browbeating and insulting the laundress's girl, accusing her of trying to get between herself and the man–cook.

"All this is very useless and disagreeable," she said, rising to go. "Good–bye, Madame Elaguine."

But Sacha laid her hand on Miss Brown's arm.

"I see," she said, "your friend and former master Mr Perry has been entertaining you with anecdotes of my life, and perhaps Edmund Lewis has been doing so also. Very shocking, weren't they? Well, I won't insult you any longer with my presence. But I think it's as well that you should know in time that if I have been in the mud according to your ideas, Walter Hamlin has been into it with me. It's rather difficult to make such things clear to a Madonna of the Glaciers, but perhaps Mr Perry will help you to understand the matter. To put it plainly, ever since you fell ill, Walter has been my lover."

The little woman spoke in a very low but very distinct voice, unabashed, brazen, almost smiling. She said the last words not in shame, but in triumph; hurled them at Anne as an outrage, almost as a thunderbolt.

"I knew it already," answered Miss Brown, gathering her white brocade skirts about her.

"You knew it!" exclaimed Madame Elaguine, staring at her as if she could not believe her ears.

"You knew it!" she repeated after a moment, a sudden triumphant scorn coming into her face. "You knew it, and you make him marry you all the same! Well, I wish you all possible happiness, and I rejoice that Walter has got a wife who understands so well how to deal with him. As to me, pray don't think that I bear you any malice. I am only surprised and amused; and extremely interested, from the psychological point of view, in finding that a virtuous woman may condescend to things which would turn the stomach of a woman who has no pretence to virtue."

Anne brushed aside the palm-leaves and ferns of the conservatory door. A sudden pain, as of a blow with the fist, was at her heart. She did not answer, for she felt that there was truth in Sacha's insult.

Miss Brown had forgotten that ignominy is an almost indispensable part of all martyrdom.

She found Hamlin standing in a little knot of friends.

"I fear I must be going home rather early," he said, "as I set off for the Italian lakes tomorrow morning, and all my packing still remains to be done. And I think," he added, with a kind of supplicating look, "that Miss Brown looks rather tired also, and ought to let me escort her home."

Anne nodded. She saw the burly shoulders, the bushy black head of Richard Brown in the crowd, and she dreaded meeting him.

"Let us go," she said.

But as they were turning away, Richard made his way to his cousin.

"Good evening, Annie," he said, in an off-hand voice; "I have had no opportunity of congratulating you and Mr Hamlin."

"Thank you, Dick," answered Miss Brown, her eyes mechanically avoiding his. "I'm sorry it's so late; the carriage is at the door, and Mr Hamlin and I must be leaving."

"Ah, very good!" said Brown. "Well, then, I will take you down, and help you to get your wraps, while Mr Hamlin finishes taking leave of his friends." He gave a contemptuous nod to Hamlin, waited for Anne to have said good-bye to her friends, and pushed his way with her through the crowd, while Mrs Argiropoulo murmured, for the thirtieth or fortieth time that evening—

"Well, I must say it is a satisfaction to see two people who are really made for each other, like Walter Hamlin and dear Anne."

There was no one as yet in the highly æsthetic study, which had been turned into a perfect exhibition of fantastic shawls and opera-cloaks. They had said nothing while going down-stairs, and even now Richard Brown was silent, as he hunted about for his cousin's cloak.

"Anne, are you there?" asked Hamlin's voice from the corridor.

Richard Brown's heavy brows contracted. "Here's your fan," he said, stooping to pick it up. "Good-bye, Nan! I hope you may be happy—"

She stretched out her hand. "Good-bye, Dick!" said Miss Brown, raising her eyes shyly upon him; "you have been very good to me—"

Richard looked at her for a moment as she stood under the lamp, in her shimmering white dress. Then, as she was going away on Hamlin's entrance, he turned round suddenly to her and murmured, in his hot angry whisper—

"Good-bye, Nan—you mercenary creature!"

A few intimate friends had assembled near the hall door, to say good-bye.

"Here, Mr Chough," cried fat old Mr Saunders, the impeccable disciple of Fra Angelico, "you'll be just in time to write a nice bridal ode while Miss Brown packs her boxes to-morrow. Mind you cut out Spenser and Suckling and all the rest of them, old boy."

Cosmo Chough, his cat-like black whiskers brushed fiercely over a shirt fantastically frilled and starched, to show his eighteenth-century proclivities, made one of his beautiful bows.

"Some better poet than I must write that ode," he said; "all that her poor servant Cosmo can do, is to thank Miss Brown from all his heart for marrying his dearest friend."

Anne heard the voice of the Poet of Womanhood vaguely, distantly, like all the others.

"Is the carriage there, Mr Hamlin?" she asked.

"Here it is. Good night! Good-bye!" cried Hamlin. He jumped in after her.

"Oh, Anne! that you should really have loved me all this time—you, really you; and that I should never have understood it," he whispered, pressing her hand, as the carriage rolled off.

"Are you cold, my love?"

Miss Brown suddenly shivered, as he put his arm round her shoulder. The flash of a street lamp as they passed quickly, had shown her Hamlin's face close to her own, and radiant with the triumph of satisfied vanity.

Printed in the United States
68180LVS00005B/73